CLAN CORMAC

ROBERT JAMES CARMACK

ARCHWAY
PUBLISHING

Cover design by BespokeBookCovers.com

Archway Publishing books may be ordered through booksellers or by contacting:

Archway Publishing
1663 Liberty Drive
Bloomington, IN 47403
www.archwaypublishing.com
844-669-3957

ISBN: 978-1-6657-0375-8 (sc)
ISBN: 978-1-6657-0376-5 (e)

Library of Congress Control Number: 2021904126

Print information available on the last page.

Archway Publishing rev. date: 3/24/2021

CONTENTS

INTRODUCTION

Humankind has forever stood upon the face of the planet and stared off into the heavens questioning his significance. Any person who has stood at the edge of the Grand Canyon or the precipice of Niagara Falls or any shore of any ocean across the globe has pondered this question. One can enter any desert around the planet and walk for a thousand miles seeing only desolation, or stand before mountain ranges so vast and so tall that the tops are capped permanently in snow or forever shrouded by clouds. We find rivers so swift and so long and oceans so deep and so vast that we wonder if we could ever possibly travel them from end to end. We ponder what extraordinary curiosities we might find if only we could summon the courage to take the first step of an unknowable venture.

In all this vast, wondrous terrain, we look at ourselves as tiny pieces that dwindle in importance and ask what difference we can make? What can one person do that might have any impact on the magnificence around us?

We are here on this earth for only a short while and thus unable to understand what role we play in the lives of other people and the planet.

A person may bring one child into existence or perhaps many children but, no one can know how those lives may play out into the future. Even if one has no children, that singular life can still have an inestimable effect upon others.

Those who first attempted to cultivate crops in antiquity stand side by side with farmers throughout the ages providing the sustenance that drives both themselves and others onward to places and deeds that would otherwise be unattainable.

The person who gives care and aid to the sick or ailing may not understand that someone they assisted might have gone on to future greatness only because of that same care that the giver dismissed as insignificant at the time.

The teacher who encourages a child to think and dream and forever seek a future unseen by others becomes larger than their own existence.

Throughout the ages, the soldiers who willingly or not spilled their blood or gave their life on land near their home or some faraway battlefield may never realize that others were spared due to that same ultimate sacrifice.

So humans go about their toil of living, unsure of what their legacy will be. One can only look back at history to find that our destinies are intertwined in intricate and inexplicable ways.

This is the story of one innocent orphaned child, grown into manhood, who could never have foreseen how his existence would cascade down through the ages, forever intersecting and interweaving amongst the intricate web of humanity.

AUTHOR COMMENT

This story was inspired after receiving a family genealogy report from a distant relative that traced our family history back before the civil war. It included an account of my great-great-grandfather, who was wounded and later died as a result of it during the civil war. I thought that it might make for an interesting subject to follow my family's journey.

Many books have been written over the years following both real and fictional families, such as East of Eden or The Grapes of Wrath by John Steinbeck, James Clavell's Shogun, and Tai Pan or The Thornbirds by Colleen McCullough. There were two that particularly stood out in my mind, James Michener's epic and sprawling Centennial and one that set the imaginations of millions across the nation afire, Roots: The Saga of an American Family by Alex Haley.

Inspiration was also found in the various television programs tracing family histories back through the generations. It remains fascinating to see someone's ancestry traced back through time to faraway places, historical events, and famous figures.

Through all of these various inputs came the decision to form a story of my family but with more fictional than real ancestral characters. So while this story does include an accounting of my two times great grandfather's life, alas, the rest is wholly summoned from my imagination.

I have taken my fictional family ancestors and placed them into actual historical events while interacting with real historical figures that I have attempted to describe with some sense of accuracy.

By inserting my characters, I in no way want to diminish those who were present at these moments, only to bring light to what is today often overlooked events and people from both our near and distant past.

Robert James Carmack January 2019

"THERE WAS NEVER YET AN
UNINTERESTING LIFE. SUCH A THING
IS AN IMPOSSIBILITY. INSIDE THE
DULLEST EXTERIOR, THERE IS A
DRAMA, A COMEDY, AND A TRAGEDY."

MARK TWAIN

IRELAND 908 AD
SAINT CORMAC

In the year 908AD, Ireland found itself separated into a handful of kingdoms, each of which is loosely comprised of many smaller ones. These smaller kingdoms number nearly one hundred and fifty and, on average, are composed of roughly three thousand people. The various kings and tribal clan leaders are frequently at war with their neighbors. Alliances and pacts are made, then broken, and then reconstructed regularly.

Cormac mac Cuilennian was an Irish Bishop named King of Munster, thus becoming the first religious and temporal leader of Ireland. He was known as a scholarly man, reading and writing in English, Greek, Hebrew, and Latin. He was a devoutly pious man, sworn to a life of celibacy and revered by all who encountered him.

He led his army of several thousand men onto the battlefield at Bellaghmoon against King Flan of Meath. During the battle, he was thrown from his horse, and his neck was broken. His enemies lopped off his head from his body and paraded it around the battlefield atop a ten-foot pike, and the battle was lost.

As the wounded were tended to and the dead carted off for

burial in the aftermath of the conflict, a small child wandered amid the carnage. The boy, not yet at the age of three, stopped at each body he came upon. Kneeling, he brushed dirt, mud, and blood from the faces of the dead men studying each for a moment before moving on to the next.

Hours later, the boy sat atop the still-warm body of a mighty brown horse just recently dead from wounds it had suffered during the battle. The boy surveyed the scene before him with an uncomprehending stare and watched as the sun darkened over him.

A nobleman wearing a blood-spattered cloak about his body slid off of his mount and, with one hand, plucked the child up in the air. Holding him at arm's length, he turned him to and fro for a good look. The child, as it had all day, made no cry as it stared into the man's black eyes. The boy was passed to an older woman for keeping until another two days had passed, and the nobleman returned.

The man now wore a fine outfit of bright shiny light chainmail. A large plume of bright red feathers adorned his helmet, and a matching red sash was draped across his chest. He asked the older woman about the child and was only mildly surprised to find out that no parents could be found neither alive nor dead. The woman shared that the boy seemed normal, perhaps a bit underfed and not very talkative but healthy enough. Since the boy had no known name and could not or would not communicate any information about the matter, the nobleman decided to give the lad a new name.

He knelt on one knee, his left hand grasping the hilt of his broadsword, and his right hand made the sign of the cross as he lifted his face in silent prayer. He stood up and stated, "I shall name him in honor of our beloved King. Henceforth this lad shall be known as Angus Cormac, and he shall live under my protection."

Young Angus grew up stout and true with a thick trunk

and massive arms; soon he would find work in a small forge working iron. At fifteen, he married a young lassie, and they soon welcomed a son, Aidan MacCormac, the Mac indicating son of Cormac. In all, the couple would bring six male and two female offspring into the world. One of the boys and both of the girls would be taken in infancy by illness and disease.

The five remaining sons named Aidan, Aidrian, Niall, Ronan, and Rodnan would each leave home to find their separate ways out in the world. Each would leave a legacy that would last long after their earthly departure.

"YOU'VE GOT TO DO YOUR OWN
GROWING, NO MATTER HOW TALL
YOUR GRANDFATHER WAS."

IRISH PROVERB

WATERFORD, IRELAND 949
DONNAL MACCORMAC, SON OF AIDAN, GRANDSON OF ANGUS

Aidan MacCormac, the eldest son of Angus, had a restless spirit that somehow led him to Waterford's port city along Ireland's southern coast. The city was a Viking settlement controlled by Norse invaders, and Aidan settled down with a fine young wife, and they soon had four sons of their own.

The eldest son of Aidan was Donnal, who was nearly as tall as his father, although not yet quite as stout at fifteen. With his father's blessing, he joined the crew of a Viking long-ship sailing for Iceland.

Three years later, in Breidafjord, Iceland, the now strapping Donnal left one of the many inns that purveyed women and ale near the port. Satisfied and smiling, he took a deep breath of the salty sea air and began walking between the roughly hewn logs that made up the various structures until a brawny fellow stepped out to block his path. Three others flanked the man, and their leader taunted Donnal as an Irish dog unworthy of Viking women and ordered him to bow down before true Norse Gods.

Donnal assessed the situation quickly and, without hesitation, charged into the leader and knocked him to the ground. His sudden attack had thrown them into disarray, and he briefly held the advantage. Their numbers took a toll, and the tide turned in their favor. As his energy drained, more of their blows hit home as he valiantly withstood their assault. Donnal rose to his feet, staggered, and landed a blow that dropped one of his attackers. He spun to fend off an attack he only sensed coming from behind.

In a roar, this attacker passed by and bludgeoned the group leader to the ground with his fists. He lifted another off of the ground, used his head as a battering ram to the man's face, and then slammed him back to the ground amid a warlike bellow. The other attackers fell back from their onslaught, grabbed their fallen fellows, and stumbled away.

With blood streaming from a gash over his eye and running through his wild red beard, the red-headed stranger grinned wildly as he turned to look at Donnal. The man slapped his hand down mightily on Donnal's shoulder and shouted, "Well done."

Donnal guessed the man to be perhaps ten years his elder, and he replied as the man began walking away, "Donnal MacCormac, sir."

The man turned, "Erik Thorvaldson," was his reply.

Donnal flashed a smile, for he had heard tales of this young Viking warrior called Erik the Red. Erik's father had been born in Norway but had murdered a man there and subsequently was banished. Now Erik had killed two men and was himself to be expelled from Iceland for three years. Erik had heard of the discovery of islands to the west of Iceland and was planning to sail to them. Donnal decided then and there to join him if he could.

The following day Donnal made his way into a tented structure set atop a wooden floor. Men stood in line before a large table with a behemoth of a man seated behind it. When his turn came, Donnal approached and stated his desire to be a part of the

expedition crew. The man staring back behind a red beard with streaks of white flowing through it seemed unimpressed. Donnal stated that he knew Erik, and while it was a slight embellishment on his part, he felt it was warranted.

The words were no sooner out of his mouth when the gigantic man shoved the solid oaken table aside as if it were a child's toy. The man may have looked large when seated but, as he rose to his feet, Donnal was taken aback. He had seen many large fellows in his days but none so massive as this man who now took a step towards him.

The giant reached out his right hand to the side without taking his eyes off of Donnal and snatched up an oaken shaft nearly four inches in circumference and, with a flick of his wrist, lifted it into the air. Twisting his hand, he caught the staff near its center and twirled it around. At its base was a large block of hardened black volcanic rock. The mammoth beast swung it in a mighty arc and slammed it to the floor inches from Donnal's unflinching feet. The fearsome man looked down at Donnal, inspecting him much as a small child might an unusual insect.

Just then, the flaps of the tent parted, and Erik sauntered in, looked around, and then up at this giant man before stating with a laugh, "Ragnall, I see you've met my friend MacCormac. Don't kill him just yet."

In such fashion, Donnal became part of Erik's crew as they sailed west from the Snaefellnes Peninsula in 982. They found land, sailed south around the southern tip of its mass, and then up the southwest coast. For two more years, they explored the areas around the south tip of the perpetually ice-covered island and established settlements as they went. As his banishment ended, they returned to Iceland, and Erik pronounced this new land to be Greenland. He wanted to bring people there to settle this forbidding place, thus giving it a more pleasant-sounding name.

He assembled a new fleet of twenty-five ships to sail west and enlarge the existing settlements and start new ones. Some of the boats were lost in the raging North Atlantic waters, and still, others turned back. Only fourteen of the ships and some five hundred settlers arrived in 986.

Originally just two colonies were established, but they would eventually grow to more than five thousand people over large areas and many fjords. Erik became the Paramount Chieftain of Greenland and built a large estate while growing wealthy and revered. He and his wife Thjodhildr now had four children, a daughter and three sons. The second of the sons claimed Donnal as his uncle even though Donnal was barely ten years older; the child's name was Leif Ericksson.

Donnal would sail with Leif from Greenland to Norway in the year 1000, stopping in the Hebrides Islands where Leif would have a son with a local chieftains' daughter. In Norway, King Olaf I would convert Leif, Donnal, and most of his crew to Christianity. One year later, they would set sail on a return voyage to spread the word of Christianity to Greenland.

Leif would follow an old Icelandic trader's tale and sail to a new land that Leif would call Vinland on this return trip. He named it thus, owing to the abundant wild grapes. They also found fields of wheat and forests of trees. They would build a small settlement there called Leifsbuoir (Leif's Booths). The following year loaded with grapes and timber, they returned to Greenland, never to return. Five hundred years later, this land would again be "discovered" by Portuguese explorers.

In 1002 more immigrants came from Iceland, and with them came disease. As the epidemic raged across Greenland, Erik the Red fell sick and died. Donnal, too fell ill but somehow survived. Leif lived through the wide-ranging pestilence with few ill effects and would not die until some twenty years later.

In the intervening years, Donnal and his two sons Fionnbarr (Fair Head) and Lochlainn (Lock-Lin) would set sail with Erik's

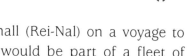

trusted second in command Ragnall (Rei-Nal) on a voyage to strange and distant lands. They would be part of a fleet of eighteen ships that would sail past England, around Gibraltar, and into the Mediterranean Sea.

The fleet would make stops for trading in many ports along the way. They would stay in Algiers for ten days, Tunis for five, and then across to Palermo on the island of Malta for two months. In Greece, they would stay in Kalamata and Athens for extended periods. They would sail across the Aegean Sea to Izmir's Turkish port, where they would stay setting up the trading business for three months. Then it was up the Turkish coast through the Aegean Sea and up towards the Sea of Marmara with another stay at Gallipoli. Here they stayed hugging the shore as they headed for their ultimate destination in Constantinople, where they would be welcomed to great fanfare as had other Viking traders for nearly two hundred years.

Constantinople had come into being in the year 324 AD when Emperor Constantine the Great had moved his government from Rome to Byzantium. He renamed it Nova Roma or New Rome, but the city became known as Constantinople or Constantine. The city was a bastion of Christianity that had defended Europe from Islam's threats ever since its' founding.

The city was an incredible fortress, a chain of massive walls stretching nearly forty miles barred entrance across the Thracian Peninsula. The walls stood some fifty-four feet tall. Just over a mile away was another wall built earlier by Constantine during the city's founding. The city was bounded by the Marmara Sea and The Golden Horn, a body of water so named for its shape, with yet more massive stone walls rising from the seafloor. Built upon seven hills was an impressive array of palaces of which the Great Palace of Constantine was preeminent.

The travelers joined the city's nearly six hundred thousand population and rapidly had a thriving trading business going.

Ragnall especially was feted for his mammoth size and was invited to the Emporers' Great Palace on more than one occasion. Even though he was now more than fifty years old, he was still a formidable man and was invited to display his battle skills at the Hippodrome.

The Hippodrome was an immense structure capable of holding one hundred thousand spectators for chariot racing and many other sporting and social events. The race track was wide enough that eight chariots could race side by side, each pulled by a team of four horses. The track was lined with bronzed statues of horses and their drivers, along with famous warriors, statesmen, Gods, and emperors alike.

Ragnall and Donnal rode into the massive stadium before the wildly cheering crowd. Their chariots stopped near the center Serpent column directly across from the Imperial box, and Ragnall stepped off holding a double-headed axe in one hand and his nine-foot long oaken shaft with a massive stone at its end in the other. He held the hammer aloft as the assembled multitudes cheered. Donnal carried a silver and bronze shield with his broadsword strapped beneath it; he also carried a double-headed axe as he stood shoulder to shoulder with Ragnall.

Amid the sounding of trumpets and drums' beating, three chariots entered the arena and raced past the two Viking warriors before skidding to a stop amid clouds of dust. Six African warriors stepped out of the dust as the crowd ooohed and aaahed. Each of the men was as black as the darkest night; they all stood tall, taller even than the giant Ragnall. They differed from his massive size with their slender, sinewy frames. Each wore a brightly colored sash, animal skin loincloths, and a single fabric swatch wrapped around one ankle. They each carried a long spear in their right hand and in their left a small round shield made of animal skin with designs of many colors upon them. Their left hand also held a second long spear.

The six men spread out in a semi-circle and began advancing.

They jumped forward three paces, pounded their spears against their shields three times, and shouted a rhythmic chant. This move was repeated twice more to the merriment of the crowd. The man on the farthest left flank let out a high-pitched war cry and let loose his spear into the air.

Ragnall dropped to one knee as the tip of the spear grazed his right shoulder. Donnal raced forward, dodging first one, then another spear. Donnal swung his axe in a wide looping arc as one warrior attempted to jab his spear through his meager defenses. Donnal's shield deflected the spear as he spun, and his axe caught the man above the left knee, and amid a spray of blood, he fell to the ground clutching in desperation to a leg that was no longer there.

Ragnall bellowed fiercely and charged at the two closest to him. He swung his mighty war hammer and the axe at the same time. The axe impaled itself in one enemy warrior while the hammer slammed into the other, throwing his broken body ten paces away.

Donnal's shield shuddered as a spear sliced through the bronze and embedded itself into his wrist. He shook off the shield and the spear with it; forgetting the injury, he charged forward, swinging his sword to ward off spear thrusts.

Just then, a series of mighty horn blasts sounded, and chariots dashed out into the midst of the fray. They formed themselves into barriers between the combatants, calling an end to the battle. The chariots pulled back to reveal Ragnall and Donnal side by side facing the three remaining African warriors as more trumpet blasts signaled an end to the festivities.

Donnal and his sons decided to remain in the city as Ragnall, and the others sailed once more on the return voyage to their distant homes. Donnal ran the flourishing trading business while his sons Fionnbarr and Lochlainn each spent time traveling the trade routes bringing in ever more goods for trade. Each of his sons would marry and bring many fine children into the world.

Donnal would fall ill in an outbreak of typhus that would eventually take his life, and his sons would take over the trading company. Over the years, they would increase their estate many times over, passing on this to their offspring as well.

"EVERY MAN IS GUILTY OF ALL
THE GOOD HE DID NOT DO."

VOLTAIRE

WATERFORD, IRELAND 990
BRAN MACCORMAC, SON OF
RODNAN, GRANDSON OF ANGUS

Bran MacCormac and his two youngest sons hauled in the nets containing a larger than usual catch, including at least thirty large fish and another twenty to thirty smaller ones. He had his sons toss the smallest of these back into the cold waters as he watched dark clouds gathering rapidly and the waves growing ever larger. He bade the boys stow the gear and their catch as he set course for home.

Less than half an hour later, the rains hit, and the sea tossed the small boat off course, and Bran knew better than to try to fight against the unforgiving and unrelenting seas. He made shore in an unfamiliar port some two to three miles from their home. He and his boys loaded down with their catch began the long walk towards their home village as the rain continued pouring down.

Three large men burst through a local inn's door and, while pulling their coats about them, made directly toward Bran and his sons. Several others stepped through the door but stayed beneath the overhanging roof in an apparent effort to keep dry.

Bran stopped as the three men approached. The man in the lead came within one stride of Bran before stopping, his eyes looked off in the distance, "That your boat?"

Bran simply replied, "Tis."

"Well," barked the man, "Who gave you permission to leave it on my land?"

Bran responded calmly, "I'll be back for it in the morning."

The man said dismissively, "You'll pay me now or be off with you and your boat."

Bran stepped forward until his face was mere inches from the man, "My name is Bran MacCormac, and the storm pushed us here. I will return in the morning." Bran turned to his youngest son, who carried a string of a dozen of the smaller fish over his shoulder and motioned for them. He turned back to the man and extended his hand that now held the stringer of fish, "Here, take these as your night's rent."

The man sneered, "Not enough, it'll take all the fish you have or take your boat away with you."

Bran dropped the rope and the fish into the mud, "There's your payment, take it or leave it." Bran turned and began walking, his boys doing their best to keep up with his long strides.

A mighty thump sounded as a large rock struck Bran in the middle of his back, and he fell to his knees.

"I'll have your head, and then I'll eat all of your fish and take your boat."

Bran rose to his feet and spoke to his sons without taking his eyes off of the three men, "Stay here boys, I'll be back shortly."

Bran picked up the rock and walked steadily and quickly towards the three men who now spread apart. The leader in the center drew a short sword from under his cloak and waved it menacingly, "Come and get it, boy."

The other two men held only small, dull knives in their hands, and all three men grinned wickedly at their overwhelming odds.

Once the distance between them had closed to fifteen feet,

Bran began charging at the man on the right, who was the largest of the three. At five feet, he threw the rock, hitting the man squarely on the nose. The man dropped his knife and, bellowing in pain, fell to his knees as Bran barreled into him and drove him to the ground while in the same motion grabbing the dull knife off the ground.

Bran jumped to his feet as the sword slashed over his head. The swordsman flailed left and right with little skill and waning enthusiasm as Bran dove at him, ignoring the hilt of the blade striking down upon his shoulder. The man fell back with Bran's full weight driving him down and knocking the wind from his lungs. Bran thrust the dull knife up through the soft skin under his chin and drove it until it would go no further.

Bran rolled off the lifeless man in time to see the third man running off in the distance. Bran turned toward the crowd of onlookers, who quickly turned and headed back inside, closing the door behind them.

Bran slowly walked back to his boys, and in silence, they walked home.

"IF YOU WANT A PLACE IN THE
SUN, YOU MUST LEAVE THE
SHADE OF THE FAMILY TREE."

OSAGE SAYING

WATERFORD IRELAND 1012
ALFRED MACCORMAC, SON OF BRAN, GRANDSON OF RODNAN

lfred lived just outside of Waterford, where he worked the land as a farmer to support his growing family. In the year 1000, he was called into service at Brian Boru's request. Brian would eventually become acknowledged as the first true King of Ireland after more than twenty years of military campaigns.

Alfred led a small contingent of soldiers numbering nearly two hundred, which included thirty mounted cavalrymen. Many of his men were experienced fighters with up to thirty years of battlefield exposure, and they tried to train those who had never held a sword or swung it in anger and with evil intent. Alfred and his men were on the march north toward Dublin amid thousands of Brian Boru's armed soldiers.

Although Brian Boru was now the sole high king of Ireland, many clans still harbored ill will, and some were slow to accept him. Among those was Sigtrygg Olaffson, the king of Dublin and better known as Sigtrygg Silkenbeard. The two kings' armies had met in battle many times over the past two decades without a

decisive victory for either side. Their forces would meet again in April of 1014 at Clontarf, near Dublin.

The corps were spread across a vast battlefield where small groups such as the one led by Alfred would clash with their rivals. Alfred had just been reinforced and now numbered over three hundred men in his command as they camped on a hillside beneath a small stand of trees. Two small brooks meandered through the valley below them. He and his men rested as mounted sentries patrolled the nearby lands for any sign of enemy activity or attack.

A rider came in with news of some five hundred men approaching from the east, and Alfred quickly formed up his men. Although outnumbered by nearly two to one, he held the advantage of the high ground. He sent a rider off to apprise Brian Boru of their situation and imminent battle.

Now into his seventies, the aged king rested in a large tent as any number of riders came and went with details of the day's battles and orders for their commanders. Brian's son Murchad was also out in the field, commanding the main forces in the battle. Alfred knew there would be no reinforcements and that he and his men would be on their own in this fight.

Alfred sat atop his mount and surveyed the scene as the enemy forces got into position and readied themselves for an attack. One hundred men on foot began to march up the hillside towards their position as Alfred led an equal number of his men to meet them.

As the two lines met, Alfred dismounted and joined in the fray. Swords clashed, and he pushed forward, slashing at the man nearest to him. His blade found unprotected flesh and bone, and blood sprayed forth as the man bellowed out in pain. Alfred moved on, driving the tip of his sword through the meager leather and wood shield of his next opponent. The man twisted the shield and flung it aside as Alfred's weapon was wrenched from his hand and the two men met, now grappling with their bare hands for the advantage. Fingers clawed and scratched for any advantage as they rolled over the ground. Alfred's hand found a discarded piece of shiny metal from someone's battle armor and scooped it into his grasp. He used it to bludgeon the man with a series of blows to the head until the man, now bloodied and battered, chose to scramble away.

The enemy commander ordered his men to withdraw. The engagement had lasted only minutes, yet each side had a dozen dead, twice that many grievously wounded and many others with lesser injuries. Both lines reformed and prepared for another attack. Alfred directed his men from above during two subsequent assaults. Sensing the time was most opportune, Alfred ordered an all-out attack. This counter-attack broke the line, and their enemies fled in total disarray in all directions.

Even as Alfred and his contingent of men were winning their encounter, Brian Boru lay resting as a group of nearly twenty riders converged upon his tent. These soldiers were of Silkenbeard's army, and when they realized who was in the tent, they attacked his meager bodyguard contingent. After overwhelming his protectors, they surrounded the aged King as he lay in bed, staring at them defiantly. His captors pulled him from the bed, and without comment, they beheaded the High King of Ireland.

Brian's son Murchad was killed in the fighting at another site, although his forces continued to fight and ultimately won the day.

Alfred would return to his home desirous of leaving the battlefields behind forevermore. He wanted to listen to the laughter of his children and the singing of his wife, not the war cries of soldiers or the sound of steel falling upon flesh and bone. He wanted more of the joy of life instead of the agony and misery of death.

CONSTANTINOPLE 1080
NIALL MACCORMAC, SON OF BRANDEN, GRANDSON OF LOCHLAINN, A DESCENDANT OF AIDAN

Niall MacCormac was the youngest of twelve children, and although only sixteen, he was tall and robust. He and three of his older brothers traveled a trade route between Samarkand and Isfahan in Persia when they came across a large caravan encamped for the night. Here they found a roaring fire and perhaps as many as one hundred men arrayed in a circle around one man at the center. He was a wizened old man with a silky white beard, and he sat on soft silken cushions drinking wine from a bejeweled silver chalice. Niall and his brothers moved closer, and introductions were made; thus, they came to meet with the Persian mathematician, scientist, astronomer, and philosopher, Omar Khayyam.

The great man tried to explain a mathematical problem using algebraic and geometric solutions, but it was lost on young MacCormac. A man among the assembled crowd asked for a poem, and all grew still and quiet. Omar Khayyam stroked his beard as if in contemplation and then began with a simple four-line quatrain;

> "All my companions, one by one died,
> With the Angel of Death, they now reside,
> In the banquette of life, same wine we tried,
> A few cups back, they fell to the side."

Heads nodded wisely, and another man asked, "Please master, another." He smiled, nodded slightly, and began:

> "The caravan of life shall always pass,
> Beware that is fresh as sweet young grass,
> Let's not worry about what tomorrow will amass,
> Fill my cup again, for this night will pass, alas."

At that, he arose, bade his goodbyes, and retired to his tent.

Two years later, Niall was out on yet another trading expedition with some twenty others when they were set upon and attacked by nearly three times their number of Varangian Guards.

The Varangian Guard had long been the emperors' bodyguard, fierce warriors based out of Constantinople. They were a force that consisted of Norse, Viking, Rus, and Anglo-Saxons known for their honor, loyalty, and also their skillful and unyielding battlefield demeanor.

Niall and his men fought off the first attack with minimal losses to his men and at least a score dead on the other side. A second attack by the Varangians left each side with less than a dozen able-bodied men. Niall led his beleaguered and battered men on an assault that ended in their total victory as they left no enemy alive.

Two days later, five hundred mounted cavalrymen encircled Niall and his five remaining men as they stood defiantly awaiting their deaths. Instead, the Varangian commander applauded their valiant fight, giving them all the possessions of those they had slain in battle, and Niall was appointed as a captain in the Guard. Niall and his descendants would continue with dual roles as traders, merchants, and now also as Varangian Guardsmen.

"THERE IS NOTHING NEW
IN THE WORLD EXCEPT THE
HISTORY WE DO NOT KNOW."

HARRY S. TRUMAN

CONSTANTINOPLE 1202
BRENDAN MACCORMAC, SON OF ALTAIR, A DESCENDANT OF AIDAN

rendan MacCormac stood as a Captain of the Varangian Guard tasked with defending Constantinople's great city against the imminent attack.

In 1198 Pope Innocent III began calling for another crusade to free the Holy lands once more. An Italian count, Marquis Boniface of Montferrat, organized a contract with Venice, the master mariners of their day. They readily agreed to build a fleet of ships counting fifty war galleys and three to four hundred supply ships to carry the crusading armies into battle. Nearly thirty-five thousand crusaders consisted of some five thousand knights and their squires and another twenty thousand foot soldiers.

Simultaneously, the Byzantine Empire was in disarray between 1180 and 1202. More than fifty rebellions or uprisings had occurred across the empire—many lay claims to the emperors' crown and the treasures and power bestowed upon its possessor.

When the crusading army sailing upon the Venetian ships

approached Constantinople's city, they were awestruck by the seemingly impregnable walls. They feared there could be no way to attack the city successfully. Indeed their first attempts were repulsed by much smaller forces. After much political intrigue and betrayal, the vacuum of a true leader spelled doom for the Orthodox Christian city of Constantinople.

The crusaders attacked once more on April 12, 1204, and succeeded in scaling the sea walls using Venetian ships topped with colossal siege towers rising more than one hundred feet above the deck. The city was captured by the 13th. and for the next three days, the crusaders ruthlessly pillaged the entire city. Ancient works of art were looted or destroyed, men murdered, and women and girls raped. Nuns were violated, and Orthodox clerics mutilated and murdered. The holy churches were desecrated. The Christian city lay in ruins at the hands of Christian Crusaders.

As the city began to fall, Brendan MacCormac was ordered by his commander to lead a group of clerics, nuns, and nobles out of the city. Guiding them through tunnels beneath the famed church of Hagia Sophia or Shrine of the Holy God, they made their escape.

Brendan would lead them out and into boats during the night, and they would make their way along the southern coast of the Black Sea to the city of Trebizond. Here two former members of the imperial family took titles of Grand Commenus and Emperor, and thus the Empire of Trebizond came into being. It comprised almost all of the southern coastal regions of the Black Sea.

One year later, Brendan would make his way back to Constantinople to retrieve his family. He found that they had fallen victim to the bloodlust of the crusaders, and all had perished. He returned to Trebizond but left the Varangians to re-enter life as a trader and quickly built a lucrative and profitable business. The Silk Road made its way into Trebizond, and it soon became a valuable port for traders heading back to Europe.

Brendan made several trips to Acre, Baghdad, and Samarkand, building trade partners for his business. He also took two wives and, over the following years, fathered sixteen children. Brendan was traveling with his firstborn son William in 1214, going from Acre across the desert in a mighty caravan heading to Baghdad, when he came upon a slave auction set up in a remote desert oasis.

He was curious about the many young fair-skinned children being auctioned and decided to participate. He bought a young boy of eleven who never spoke even when given the lash. Brendan's son William was more gentle and treated the young slave with kindness until three days later; the boy finally broke his silence.

He gave his name as Martine and that he had been part of a great crusade. Brendan laughed, but William bade him continue with his story. He claimed that in May of 1212, he had joined with Stephen of Cloyes on his crusade to recapture Jerusalem. Stephen was a twelve-year-old boy who stated that God had chosen him to lead an army of children to reclaim the holy lands. Martine claimed to be just one of many thousands, perhaps as many as thirty thousand children, who joined Stephen as he marched throughout France. Many parents proudly and eagerly sent their little ones off to participate in this holy quest.

Many died due to the hardships on the trek, and as a result, only a few thousand made it to Marseilles' coastal town. They prayed that the seas would recede before them as they had for Moses, but this blessed event never occurred. Finally, two Christian merchants offered up their ships to take the children to Palestine. Seven vessels set sail with as many children as they could carry. The ships sailed instead to the Algerian coast, where all the children were sold into captivity there. The boy had served for a year in Egypt as a slave to a teacher who lived in Cairo. The teacher had died from illness, and once more, he was sold and had come to this desert place.

Brendan believed not a word of this tale, although he could not give a reasonable explanation for the boys' presence among them. William did not need to be convinced, and the two young men would become fast friends for the remainder of their lives.

"HISTORY NEVER LOOKS LIKE HISTORY
WHEN YOU ARE LIVING THROUGH IT."

JOHN W. GARDNER

THE SILK ROAD 1218
WILLIAM MACCORMAC, SON OF BRENDAN, A DESCENDANT OF AIDAN

William MacCormac rode across the vast grasslands with some two hundred Persian merchants and nearly one thousand heavily laden beasts heading for the cities of Karakorum and Samarkand. On the third day of their trek, as the sun reached its highest point in the sky, William stopped his horse and raised his face to the heavens. He had begun to hear a strange noise, a rumble such as from a distant storm. Soon, others in the party noticed the odd sounds as they searched the cloudless skies for signs of the impending storm.

Hour after hour, the rumbling sounds increased, yet no storm clouds appeared on the horizon. The noise ceased as the sunset, and they made camp with a sense of unease. Whispered conversations around the campfires concerned the nature of what this storm could have been. The camp arose early and was on the move long before the first light. They had been moving for an hour when the rumbling of the mighty storm began once more. The beasts grew jittery and jumpy as the roar grew slowly but steadily louder, yet still, they drove onward.

Soon the entire horizon seemed to dim amid the strange storm. The caravan halted and circled in amongst itself as a measure of protection from the approaching fury of nature. With Martine at his side, William could now feel the very ground beneath his feet tremble as the roar of thunder grew ever closer.

Shouts rang out, and all eyes moved to the east as a wave of men on horseback came over the crest of a hill. They rode in a near-perfect line with barely a single pace between each rider and the next. William tried to count their number, quickly guessing that there must be one hundred horsemen in this line. He blinked, now seeing another line even farther to the east and then another and another and another.

Spinning, he looked to the west to see similar lines of riders fanning out as far as the eye could see. As the riders' wave passed by them, he was astonished to see another row one hundred meters behind them also charging forward. He turned back and forth, estimating that each line contained some ten groups of one hundred riders or close to one thousand in all. His mind grew numb as the surge of riders passed. He sat upon the ground, finally losing count after some forty or more waves had thundered past.

A single rider holding a tall shaft with a variety of colorful pennants approached their position. William watched as the man lifted the pole high in the air. He then dipped it first to one side and then the other; he twirled it overhead and then pointed it forward. Within moments riders swooped in on all sides to surround their positions. All of the riders carried bows and quivers of arrows; some also carried javelins, scimitars, and lances. Without warning, a volley of arrows was unleashed, and a handful of the caravans' members dropped to the ground along with several animals as the riders sat still upon their mounts.

Finally, a small group of riders came into the caravan center, and a man wearing brightly colored silken clothing approached. The man had blue coloring encircling his eyes, and he bowed deeply before speaking to the group in first one language and then another. The Persian chieftains carried on a conversation with him until he waved a hand to quiet them.

He approached William, examining his reddish hair, and greeted him with a large smile. He introduced himself as an emissary of their great leader, Genghis Khan. He asked them to accompany him to meet with the Khan.

Many of their party were taken on a two-day journey to the encampment of Genghis Khan. They arrived to see a magnificent tented pavilion of pure white under which a thousand people could fit comfortably. Here Genghis sat upon a massive throne of solid gold.

They were introduced to the Khan, who generously talked of trade and goodwill among his people. They were interrupted by some commotion as one man rode through the crowd dragging a bloody and battered body behind him. The man on horseback was one of the Khans' generals, and he brought forth a leader who had refused the invitation of Genghis to surrender his forces. Now after their defeat, he was brought to the feet of his conqueror.

The man now naked, battered, and bruised knelt before the Khan, and William watched the spectacle in amazement. The man was pulled back down to the ground, and molten metal was poured into his eyes and mouth until he was dead. As the body was pulled away, Genghis waved William and his group to step forward once more to continue discussing trade agreements.

In this way, William MacCormac became a key trading partner with both the Mongol Empire and the remainder of the world, and the city of Trebizond became a central terminus of the Silk Road.

THE SILK ROAD 1272
RORY MACCORMAC, SON OF BRYON, GRANDSON OF WILLIAM, A DESCENDANT OF AIDAN

Rory had just turned twenty and was set to help his older brothers take over for his ailing father, who ran the family trading business. Rory was the youngest of seven brothers, but even so, he had made many trips over the years, continuing the long tradition of trading across vast stretches of the famed Silk Road. He was nearing the Persian city of Tabriz when they met up with another party traveling a similar route.

The group was led by brothers Niccolo and Maffeo Polo from the Italian city of Venice. In the party was Niccolo's' son Marco barely eighteen years old. They had begun their journey with some six hundred men but now numbered less than twenty, and they required guides to help them continue on their journey. Rory struck up a friendship with Marco and soon volunteered his services to lead the expedition.

Their journey would take nearly three more years to fulfill their request to return to China and the court of Kublai Khan. He was Khagan or Great Khan, leader of the Mongols and Emperor of China. He had completed his conquest of the Sung Dynasty and then brought his capital from Karakorum in Mongolia to Taitu in China. They would meet with Kublai Khan at his summer palace in Shangdu or Xanadu in the year 1275.

The city lay amid lush green rolling hills and valleys where cool breezes made the summer temperatures pleasant. It was square in its layout with an outer city housing some one hundred thousand residents and an imperial city inside that for use by imperial officers conducting the business of running the empire. Then there was the palace city, a rectangular brick structure where the Khan and his wives lived. The walls surrounding the town were made of earth and fortified with stone and served as home to soldiers standing sentry on the battlements.

The city contained over one hundred temples, and the imperial palace was made with the finest marble. The palace's roof was covered in various colored tiles varnished so fine that they would shine brightly and be seen from miles away. Nearly every structure was adorned with golden dragons and magnificent gilt figurines shined from all buildings' tops. Rooms and halls were painted with depictions of all manner of men and strange or exotic beasts.

The city had a man-made system for pumping water for fountains and drainage to many structures. Great parks containing rivers, brooks, and fountains ran through rolling meadows among an astonishing variety of trees and flowering plants, each precisely laid out upon the grounds with meticulous care. Hundreds of falcons and hawks were cared for, and the sport was highly encouraged by the Khan.

The group would stay here with the Khan for the summer months, and then as autumn came and the Khan was about to move on, he asked Marco to go to the North toward the traditional Mongolian homelands. Rory would go South to undertake a journey to observe his armies in their attack upon Japan's island.

Two months later, Rory stood transfixed as he marveled at

the sight of some one hundred and forty thousand troops that would board ships and sail off from two directions to converge upon the island of Kyushu. A typhoon struck the fleet, and more than half of the troops were either lost or captured. The Japanese believed a Kamikaze or Divine Wind had been delivered to them. After this disastrous undertaking, the Chinese forces withdrew, and Rory traveled up the Yangtze River, talking to merchants at Kublai Khan's request.

This trek lasted for more than three years until he reached Tibet. He then headed in a Northwesterly direction for two more years before reaching Karakorum. He spent nearly six months relaying details of his journey to the Khans courtiers prior to setting out on his return home to Trebizond some ten years after leaving.

"It is forbidden to kill; therefore all murderers are punished unless they kill in large numbers and to the sound of trumpets."

VOLTAIRE

FRANCE 1280

BRYAN, RONALD, ROGER, EDWARD MACCORMAC, SONS OF LIAM, GRANDSON OF BRONNARD, DESCENDANTS OF NIALL

ryan MacCormac was a small sickly child when born, and his situation only seemed to worsen during his first two years of life. His father developed a ragged cough that sounded wet and raw, and he soon began bringing blood up with every convulsion. His death only made the families' struggle that much more difficult. Bryan had three older brothers and three older sisters, and they held tightly to each other as a safe haven in an otherwise cruel and harsh world.

His brothers were; Ronald, two years older, Roger four years older, and Edward, the eldest of the boys just five years older. The people of their village rarely saw one without the other three in close company. Bryan eventually grew tall and strong, and by the age of ten, he was often mistaken as the eldest of the clan. By fifteen years of age, Bryan appeared as a man with a scraggly and patchy beard, and his brothers were equally as rough and ragged as he.

The boys joined in amongst a large gathering of several hundred; indeed, it was the most people any of the boys had ever seen in one place and at one time. The occasion was that their liege lord, King Rodrick, had summoned everyone from the surrounding countryside to come together. A Bishop and what must surely be every priest within fifty miles were also in attendance. The boys had only seen their king twice before as he passed through their village, and now they pressed to the front of the crowd.

The Bishop spoke a benediction in Latin while the crowd anxiously awaited word from their king. Finally, Rodrick stepped forward with his arm outstretched and holding in his hand a small piece of red cloth with a white cross embroidered upon it. In a strong, clear authoritarian voice, he called out, "I seek those who would also take up the cross and join me in the name of the Holy Mother, the Virgin Mary, and our Lord God."

Shouts and cheers erupted from the crowd, and much to the surprise of his brothers, Bryan stepped forward and shouted, "I will take up the cross and join you, my king."

Edward, Roger, and Ronald, without hesitation, each stepped forward and joined their baby brother. The four were hauled up onto the makeshift platform where they knelt before their king and received a blessing from the Bishop himself. Others in the crowd pushed forward, and by the day's end, there were nearly two hundred men and boys that had pledged their immortal souls to serve God and the Blessed Virgin Mother in the battle against all those who stood opposed to King and country and God's will.

The boys were given one week to say their goodbyes and return, ready to begin their training as Sergeants at arms with the Knights Templar. When the Templars were formed in 1119, they were quartered in the Aqsa Mosque, also known as Solomon's Temple. The Knights Templar's wore white robes or surcoats marked with a red cross and a white mantle. The knight's primary duty was to fight, and since they believed that their immortal soul was protected, they were thus allowed to be fearless in battle.

The brave knights had been doing holy battle for nearly two hundred years since their founding. Initially formed to protect holy relics in Jerusalem and the pilgrims who traveled to see them, they had undergone many transformations throughout the years.

Christians had long believed that a pilgrimage to the holy lands was a meaningful way to test the strength of their faith. The journey was long, arduous, and dangerous and meant that travelers needed to carry sufficient funds to support such a trek. These same travelers quickly became targets for bandits, rogues, and all those who opposed the Christians. Templars protected the pilgrims during their travels and built safe houses and castles with fortifications throughout Christendom and beyond for this purpose.

Many wealthy pilgrims were captured and held for ransom, and it was the Templar Knights who first provided a way for the holy pilgrims to travel without having to carry large amounts of coin with them. They could deposit their money with the Order near where they lived, and then upon arriving at any Templar stronghold along the way, they could withdraw their funds safely. The Templars soon became wealthier than most of the kings and kingdoms around them. It was the Order to which Kings and Popes came for funds to pay for their wars and crusades.

The brothers began nearly one full year of learning the craft of warfare and the Templars' ways, hours every day were spent in prayer and contemplation, and many more in weapons training and battlefield tactics. Each swore an oath of poverty, chastity, and obedience. As Sergeants at arms, they wore a black tunic with a red cross.

They traveled across the land, often stopping to do mock battle in elaborate faires and festivals where competing companies of knights would do battle. These battles would pit one man against another, or they might be matched in pairs. Or, as in this occasion, two score mounted knights and men at arms facing each other across an open field where hundreds of spectators had gathered to watch the violent, bloody, and quite often deadly spectacle.

Bryan and Edward were on opposite ends of the line of horsemen who stood mere inches apart. While maintaining tight formations, training in this squadron charge had been the Templar's successful formula for their two-hundred-year history. Even this relatively small number of knights still provided a fearsome sight as they began their charge forward.

The two lines crashed together as the individual combatants thrashed in violent combat. Bryan thrust his sword forward and raised his shield to thwart a spiked iron mace from knocking him off of his mount. The ball of the mace impaled itself in his triangular and lightly curved shield. One of the spikes embedded in his forearm, and he felt his blood begin flowing freely. He dropped in the saddle and thrust upward with his sword once more, it slid through a small opening, and he drove it forward through two layers of padded cloth and a thin piece of chain mail. Its wearer yelped in pain as the sword tip cut through an inch of flesh and bounced off bone before being withdrawn. The man quickly shouted, "Yield, I yield," as he slid off his mount and dropped to the ground, as did many of his companions. The Templars raised both their swords and their voices in jubilation.

ACRE NEAR JERUSALEM 1299
BRYAN MACCORMAC, SON OF
LIAM, A DESCENDANT OF NIALL

The few remaining Knights regrouped, reformed their line, and stared silently out at an enemy five times their number. Most of the Templars were wounded, at least two mortally so. Bryan, now himself a battle-hardened Templar Knight, wiped blood and sweat from his eyes and blinked to clear his head. Sir Rotherall, his commander, was bleeding profusely from a lance wound near his hip, and he grimaced in pain as his mount shifted uneasily. "Bryan, take two men and ride for the port, leave for Rhodes with the report of our valiant stand."

Bryan and two younger men-at-arms reluctantly rode off as ordered while the remaining Templars shouted out to the Blessed Virgin Mary and charged into their final battle.

Bryan would spend the next few years based upon the island of Rhodes, which had become the base for all Templar activities. His brothers Edward and Roger were now both near Bordeaux while their brother Ronald had gone to Vienna with a contingent of like-minded soldiers who belonged to the Hospitallers, an organization that mirrored the Templars in many, if not most ways.

PARIS FRANCE 1307
ROGER, RONALD, AND BRYAN MACCORMAC, SONS OF LIAM, DESCENDANTS OF NIALL

oger MacCormac traveled with his commander heading to Paris on Friday, October 13, 1307, when they awoke to find themselves surrounded and placed under arrest on King Philip's orders. Templars all over Europe were arrested and thrown into prison.

Roger was questioned about the Templar activities, and when he would not give his inquisitors the answers, they sought he was beaten and whipped. Still, his responses were not satisfactory, and he was bound hand and foot while lying upon a long table. A large wheel was slowly turned, thus pulling the ropes taut until his arms and legs were stretched to where sinew and flesh began to tear apart. Seven days after his capture Roger was tied to a post before a large jeering crowd in a town square. He listened as they stated that he had admitted to being a heretic, and he lifted his eyes to the heavens as they lit the fires that would consume his mortal flesh.

Most Templars fled or went into hiding. Some fifteen

thousand Templar houses were abandoned, and the vast Templar treasures vanished with them. Edward had returned to Rhodes and one last meeting with Bryan before setting sail for Scotland, where he and many others would find refuge. Bryan pleaded with Edward, "Come with me, my brother, we sail to safety in Portugal." Edward smiled, "No, my path must lie with my comrades at arms who are set to sail to Scotland." Bryan added, "I fear we shall never meet again, brother." Edward put his arms around his brother, "As God wills it, my brother, as God wills it."

Ronald stayed in the Swiss Alps with a large number of Templar knights. The Swiss had little if any military experience, and folk tales would later tell of armed white knights that appeared seemingly from nowhere to assist them in their battles. Indeed, Leopold I of Austria led a force of several thousand knights into the St. Gotthard Pass in an attempt to control the Swiss people, and his troops were overrun and crushed by a group of supposed peasants only one-fifth their size.

Bryan himself would sail from Rhodes to Malta in a convoy of five Templar ships. They journeyed to Portugal, where given support from Portuguese King Philip, they simply changed name from the Templars to the Military Order of Christ. Bryan would become a ship's captain sailing out of Lisbon where in between voyages, he would marry and father six children, each of whom would become tied to both the sea and The Order of Christ.

"UNTIL LIONS HAVE THEIR HISTORIANS,
TALES OF THE HUNT SHALL ALWAYS
GLORIFY THE HUNTERS."

AFRICAN PROVERB

SWISS TERRITORIES 1307
RONALD MACCORMAC, SON OF LIAM, A DESCENDANT OF NIALL

onald had now lived among the Swiss people for some years, even taking a wife who had already given him two sons named Julien and Bastien. Having settled into a comfortable life, he now set out on horseback towards the town of Burglen, intending to purchase a new dress as a surprise for his wife. Along the way, he came across a man and boy walking beside the trail and struck up a conversation.

The tall, muscular fellow carried a crossbow slung over his shoulder and greeted Ronald warmly. He introduced himself as hunter and mountain climber Wilhelm Tell and his son as Walter. Thus the three chatted amiably as they entered the town on 18 November 1307.

In the town of Burglen, bailiff Gessler representing the Count of Habsburg was visiting. Gessler had placed his hat at the end of a ten-foot-long pole in the town square and demanded that all the townsfolk would show reverence to their Austrian rulers by bowing before the hat.

Tell refused to bow to the hat, and Gessler had him arrested.

Ronald stood back among the crowd with his hand upon the hilt of his sword as Tell was brought before the bailiff. Gessler knew that Tell was famed as a marksman. Gessler announced that both Wilhelm Tell and his son were to be executed for their insolence. People in the crowd shouted out for leniency. The bailiff smiled and stated that Tell would be set free if he could shoot an apple off the top of his son's head.

Young Walter was placed up against a tree and an apple set upon his head. Wilhelm pulled two bolts from his quiver, slid one into the crossbow, and calmly took aim. Tell split the apple in two as the crowd roared.

Tell was brought once more before Gessler, who congratulated him on the shot and stated that he was curious why he had pulled two bolts out. Tell said, "If I had killed my son, the second bolt would have killed you."

Gessler flew into a rage, "I will spare your life, but you will be imprisoned in the dungeon of the castle at Kussnacht."

Tell was placed aboard Gessler's boat, and they set out across Lake Lucerne. Ronald mounted his horse and rode for the castle. Dark clouds quickly brought in a raging storm, and the guards grew fearful that the boat would sink. They begged Gessler to free Tell from his shackles so that he could take control of the vessel and lead them to safety. The bailiff reluctantly agreed, and Tell took the helm.

As the boat neared a rocky ledge, Tell leaped from the boat and raced across the countryside toward Kussnacht. Gessler and his men finally arrived and pursued Tell, who had met up with several other men, including Ronald. As they moved through a narrow pass cut through rock, Tell fired a shot from the crossbow that killed the bailiff, Gessler.

Tells' shot would spark a rebellion against the Austrian Habsburg rule that would last for several years, ultimately leading to the Swiss Confederacy's founding. Ronald took up the sword once more and fought side by side with Tell through all the battles to come.

SCOTLAND 1307
EDWARD MACCORMAC, SON OF LIAM, A DESCENDANT OF NIALL

Edward MacCormac settled in Scotland with nearly fifty other Templars as they contemplated their collective and individual futures. Less than a fortnight passed before the Templars were visited by Robert the Bruce; by now crowned as King of the Scots and under attack by the English King Edward I. Bruce's wife and sisters were captured and imprisoned in hanging cages where they would remain for several years. The king convinced the Templars to join him in his fight, and they slipped away to Ireland during the cold months of winter in 1307/1308.

Edward fought alongside Robert the Bruce in battle after battle over the next several years until the Scots secured their independence from England with a victory at the Battle of Bannockburn in 1314. The following year Edward took a wife who bore him five fine children over the next ten years. As the bitter cold of winter set in, Edward fell feverously ill and lapsed into a catatonic state. He lingered thusly for nearly ten days before passing away to his eternal sleep.

"THE SCARIEST MONSTERS ARE THE ONES THAT LURK WITHIN OUR SOULS."

EDGAR ALLEN POE

IRELAND 1349

ROGAN MACCORMAC, SON OF EDWARD, GRANDSON OF LIAM, A DESCENDANT OF NIALL

Rogan and his family of seven scratched a living from the ground and pulled fish from the sea as they enjoyed a relatively peaceful time in the Irish countryside.

Soon word came of an invisible death that was sweeping across the seas, and the villagers grew nervous. There was no hiding from the Black Death that washed over the lands.

Rogan watched helplessly as his children fell ill one by one, and within days they were gone. His broken-hearted wife also became sick and gladly gave herself over to join her beloved children. Rogan wept as he spread the dirt atop the graves of his family, and he dropped to his knees, contemplating what his future might be. He looked to the heavens for an answer as a spasm of pain in his chest brought up several coughs, each with a fine spray of blood. He lay down on the freshly tilled ground and told his family that he would join them soon.

"EVERYDAY COURAGE HAS FEW
WITNESSES. BUT YOURS IS NO LESS
NOBLE BECAUSE NO DRUM BEATS FOR
YOU OR CROWDS SHOUT YOUR NAME."

ROBERT LOUIS STEVENSON

LONDON, ENGLAND 1400
JONATHON EDWARD MACCORMAC, A DESCENDANT OF RONAN

Upon his birth, the doctor suggested to the mother that she allow him to end her newborn's life and save him from a lifetime of torment and pain. The scared, sickly, malnourished, fifteen-year-old girl, who had gone through her pregnancy alone and without support from anyone, clutched her precious infant to her chest and shook her head no.

Little Jonathon cried loudly as the young mother tried without much success to feed him from her breast. She did the best she could for her sickly child, but life was a difficult challenge for a young girl on her own, let alone one with a small child. Yet she rocked him in her loving arms and stared into his blue-green eyes while whispering sweet songs of childlike hope and wonder.

As the boy grew, she noticed that he did not use his right hand but kept it clutched tightly to his chest. He cried in earnest whenever she tried to stretch his hand and arm out straight. When he finally began crawling, it was without his right arm's support, and he scooted around on his bottom instead. She loved him all the same and never wavered in defense of her treasured charge.

Jonathon was nine years old and helping his mother with the sorting of a rather large pile of dirty clothes that she was in charge of cleaning when she dropped to her knees and called out his name. Something in the sound of her voice sent a chill down his spine as she tumbled face-first into the laundry. He turned her over and looked into her eyes as she stared back at him, unblinking. He sat and rocked her back and forth while he sang her the same songs she had once used to comfort him.

The boy stood silently as they lowered his mother's body into the ground. A man he did not know held his hand and led him away from the gravesite. The man spoke softly and reassured the boy that he would be alright, that arrangements had been made for his care. He was placed upon a cart drawn by a forlorn horse who limped as it made its way through the city.

Bethlehem Hospital had come into being more than one hundred fifty years earlier when a returning crusader knight had donated land to be the site of a hospital named for the Virgin Mary and the Star of Bethlehem. The hospital was intended to be for the healing of sick, indigent people who had no other means of care. Bethlehem Hospital was often referred to as just Bethlem' and often pronounced Bedlam. Over time it had become infamous as an asylum for the mentally deranged lunatics of the day.

Jonathon entered Bedlam and was immediately placed in a tiny room that had no window. Here he was kept in complete isolation in the belief that patients being separated from outside influences would help them to realize the errors of their ways. Jonathon did not understand why he was being punished in this way and longed for his mother's loving touch and comforting words.

Occasionally he would be dragged from the darkness, often in the middle of the night, have his clothes torn off, and then he would be dunked in icy cold water in the hopes that his body would be shocked back into a state of normalcy. On numerous instances, he was strapped to a small wooden chair that hung several inches off of the floor in the middle of the room. One of the doctors' aides would begin turning the chair until it was spinning more than one rotation per second. This would be kept up until Jonathon vomited, and he would then be forced to attempt walking in a straight line or perform other simple tasks.

These therapies were used for many years, and Jonathon suffered these treatments until he reached fifteen, and a new nurse joined the staff. Sarah was the twenty-five-year-old daughter of a wealthy shipping magnate and the wife of an influential magistrate of the court. Appalled at what she saw as abusive and often torturous conduct under the guise of imagined curative healing, she appealed to both her husband and her father to help put an end to such actions.

She was able to remove Jonathon from Bedlam and took personal responsibility for his care to the point that she brought him into her home. His health was poor, and he cried out in terror whenever anyone came close to him. It would take several weeks before he would allow her to get near enough even to touch him. She was finally able to hold his hand and soon after began to take him outside for short walks. Jonathon marveled at the sights and sounds of a world that now seemed foreign after almost six years as a virtual prisoner in a tiny dark room.

Over the next five years, Jonathon blossomed into a sweet, caring young man who could finally smile simply at the sight of his savior Sarah. His favorite thing to do was to listen as Sarah sang sweet lullabies while he dreamt of his mother from so long ago.

A cholera epidemic raged across the city, and Sarah fell ill, and it was Jonathon's turn to sit by her bed and sing softly to her. He stayed at her side night and day, stifling the cough and fever he felt brewing inside him; he kept her bedding clean, holding her hands and trying to get her to eat and drink. His care was to no avail, and after several days she closed her eyes and slipped away. Jonathon kissed her cheek as tears fell from his eyes, and then he laid his head upon her chest and joined her in the afterlife.

"WE ARE BORN, WE LIVE, AND
WE DISAPPEAR. ONE OF THE
CHILLING ASPECTS OF HISTORY IS
THE SWIFTNESS WITH WHICH IT
CARRIES US INTO OBLIVION."

DAVID EBERSHOFF

CORK, IRELAND 1406
WINIFRED MACCORMAC, DAUGHTER OF ALAIN, GRAND-DAUGHTER OF WILLIAM, A DESCENDANT OF AIDRIAN

Winifred was born in Cork along the southern coast of Ireland as the fourth of twelve offspring. Only six of the children would live to see sixteen years of age. As the eldest female, Winifred often assumed the role of mother in caring for her younger brothers and sisters, who were often in poor health. When their mother passed from pneumonia, she continued with the care of the little ones.

She soon found herself as a twenty-four-year-old, "old maid" while serving as a midwife for women in the community. She also saw to the birthing of foals, calves, ewes, and all manner of living creatures. Desperate for something more in her life, she heeded the call of her King, whose emissaries landed in port with calls to soldiers willing to join in the fight for control of France.

This war that had now lasted off and on for nearly one hundred years, once more beckoned. Where men sailed off to battle, so too were support services needed. As bloody battles were fought, there was always a steady flow of wounded and dying in need of care and comfort. Many women marched along in support of these troops. Rare were those that would wade into the areas of bitter conflict to care for those in need; of these, Winifred was one.

She risked her English lords' ire by tending to any sick or injured soul without regard to their nationality. She often drove her cart alone down unprotected lanes in search of those in need of her skills. She had set up her camp in a clearing not far from the battles taking place in Orleans when she heard the sound of riders approaching.

A dozen riders at full gallop thundered towards her. Most were knights in full battle armor; some carried tall banners that flapped in the wind. In their midst was a solitary rider clad in a white cloak with a hood draped over his head. This rider was slumped forward slightly, and as they closed the distance, Winifred could see the cloak was covered in blood near the right shoulder and chest.

The thunder of the horse's hooves stopped abruptly as the rider in front dismounted rapidly and approached Winifred. He was an older man in bloody and battered armor who asked, "Be you the caregiver we have heard spoken of?"

She affirmed that she was, and the man continued, "I beg you care for God's messenger, Joan, the Maid of Orleans."

A blanket had been spread upon the ground, and the wounded individual had been gently laid upon it. The knights took up defensive positions on all sides facing outward; many knelt to one knee and lifted their voices to the heavens in prayer.

Winifred pulled the hood off and was stunned to see a young woman looking up at her. Joan's hair was short-cropped, and she wore a man's clothing. Winifred was taken aback by the look of serenity upon the girl's face. The metal shaft of a crossbow arrow was embedded into her shoulder.

Joan had been born in Domremy in northeastern France, where she lived an everyday life as a farm girl. She could neither read nor write, although she regularly attended church services with her devout mother. At the age of twelve, she began hearing voices and seeing visions she claimed were the voices of angels and saints. By the age of sixteen, the church had confirmed the legitimacy of her claims. She went to Paris claiming that she was to lead French armies into battle to drive the English invaders from their soil once and for all and see that the Dauphine was seated upon the throne. She had led the troops into battle, directing French generals and their troops in the successful siege of Orleans.

Winifred carefully removed the arrow's shaft from the girl's shoulder and stitched the wound with great care. She was amazed that the girl had remained smiling throughout the ordeal and never cried out even once in pain.

As Winifred dressed the wound, the young Joan looked at her and spoke softly, "God bless you, my child."

A column of men rode into camp, and Joan was placed in a cart and removed from the area. Winifred never saw her again, although nearly a year later, she wept at the news that this young woman, who had been captured during battle at Compiegne and held prisoner for months, would be burned at the stake as a lapsed heretic on May 30, 1431.

Winifred grew tired of the constant battlefield trauma and left the warring behind, searching for a more peaceful existence. She finally settled in a small village outside of Paris, tending to the poor villagers with their more common variety ailments. She would never marry nor bear children, and her life slipped away after fever swept through the area taking nearly half its residents with it.

"THOUGH LOVERS BE LOST, LOVE
SHALL NOT; AND DEATH SHALL
HAVE NO DOMINION."

DYLAN THOMAS\

VENICE ITALY 1474

MICHAEL MACCORMAC, A DESCENDANT
OF BRAN, A DESCENDANT OF RODNAN

Michael helmed the wheel and shouted out orders to the crew as the ship settled into Venice's port. Badly in need of repairs since nearly going down in high seas some three weeks earlier, she limped towards the docks. Michael was only twenty years old but served as the first mate to the captain who lay below in his cabin suffering from a fever that developed after a minor cut on his leg became infected. The crew performed as required and now looked to Michael with hungry eyes and swollen loins as they waited for permission to leave the ship once they were safely docked in port.

Michael had been in many foreign ports during his twelve years at sea, the last five aboard this vessel at the command of Master Vantana, Captain of the ship, and although a stern taskmaster at sea, was also the kindest soul Michael had ever met. The captain had taken a liking to the tall redheaded boy and over the years had promoted him up to first mate even though there were older and more experienced men aboard. Reluctant at first to follow the commands of a man younger than they, he grudgingly won over their respect by his skill and his natural leadership abilities.

After seeing fresh food and supplies being replenished on board and calling for a doctor to tend to the Captain, Michael began letting men ashore for leave. He looked longingly at Venice's famed port city, a maritime empire for more than two hundred years. He knew that he must remain onboard until the Captain reclaimed the use of his faculties.

The following day the Captain was carried ashore, and Michael walked along the dock anxiously wishing he could partake of the pleasures he saw paraded before him. Three days later, the Captain's fever had broken, and he called for Michael. The Captain thanked him for his loyalty, service, and actions that had most likely saved his very life.

Two days later, Michael sauntered down the street with a pouch full of coins in his pocket, a bounce in his step, and a smile on his face. He didn't have to go far to find an establishment selling ale to a bevy of homesick and now tipsy sailors. Michael felt right at home as he raised a mug and joined in singing with several dark-skinned sailors whose language he did not understand.

In short order, Michael had the attention of more than one lady. He kissed the cheek of three or four different women before he caught a flash out of the corner of his eye and spun quickly around. The woman twisted her head, and her long black curls flashed first one way and then the other. She turned while laughing at some comment, and he saw the outline of her curvy silhouette. At long last, she spun in his direction, and he could finally see her face. She broke into a broad smile and blew him a kiss from across the room.

He grinned and motioned for her to come over. It took her ten agonizing minutes to make her way over to where he sat anxiously squirming in his seat. She leaned in close, and he detected the aroma of a wonderful floral fragrance in her hair as he closed his eyes and slipped dreamily away. Her laugh brought him back to the present. After some fleetingly whispered negotiations, which consisted of him nodding in the affirmative to whatever she said, they headed up the stairs.

Long lonely weeks at sea were rapidly forgotten as Michael lost himself in the welcome embrace of his new lover Katarina. Not wanting their time together to end, he willingly handed over his hard-earned wages to this dark-haired beauty who whispered the sweet sounds of a forever love into his love-struck ears.

Over the next five weeks, he began to dread the thought of ever leaving her side and fervently hoped for delays to the ship's repair. Each time he left the boat, his heart was light, and he raced to her arms. Each time he left her, it seemed as if his shoes were made of lead, and his heart ached. The Captain gave him a stern lecture about the dangers of falling in love with beautiful young whores in exotic ports of call, and speaking from his personal experience; he knew it would do little good to persuade the young man to pursue his love quest.

As provisions began to be loaded aboard the ship for its departure in three days, Michael came back on board and immediately sought out the Captain.

Michael blurted out, "Sir, I must remain in Venice for I am to be a father. Yes, she is with child, and I must do what is right."

The Captain calmly invited his first mate to sit and slowly poured them each a large glass of local wine he had become fond of since arriving in Venice. The Captain spoke softly in a fatherly tone, "Michael, I understand your feelings, and I condone you for wanting to do the right thing as it were." He paused while sipping from his wine, "I must speak frankly with you, although you might not find it pleasant." Michael nodded for him to continue, "But you must realize that there will be no way to know if the child is even yours until after its birth, and even then, you might not be able to tell. Although a beautiful woman and professing to love you, she is still working as a prostitute, and she lay with men other than you. I know that these words hurt your heart, but you must realize the folly of your actions."

Michael's shoulders sagged, and without raising his head, he spoke resignedly, "I understand all that may be true, but still I know what I must do."

They sat in silence while the Captain stroked his fingers about his chin, "Perhaps there is another way through this dilemma. We are due to sail in days, and you must depart with us and fulfill your duties. With only a few slight alterations to our course, we could return here in one year, perhaps less if our trading goes well."

Michael stood up smiling as the Captain continued, "At that time, you may determine if the child is yours and let the fates decide upon your future at that time."

Michael agreed to this solution. He also gathered what money he could and gladly handed it over to his beloved Katarina and bade her await his return in one year. They lay in each other's arms delaying their tearful parting as long as possible.

Michael stood at the stern of the ship as they pulled out of port, and he silently called out a vow to his unborn child that he would return to comfort and protect both child and mother forevermore.

The midwife held Katarina's hand and wiped away the perspiration from her brow as the baby made its way out of the mother by thrusting a shock of bright red hair into the world. Mother and son lay staring into each other's eyes as she whispered to him about his father and the wonderful life they would lead upon his return. She gave him the name of Filippi.

Two days later, she became fevered, and the other girls worried over her as she seemed to slip farther away from them. After a brief reprieve, her condition worsened, and a doctor was called. He never made it to her side before the new mother passed from this life, and young Filippi was left as a whore's bastard and orphaned child.

Michael stood at the helm next to the Captain, with both of them held in place by ropes stretched across the deck. Four other crewmen stood nearby and were also held in place by these lifelines. The storm raged around them as the ship was tossed about like a child's toy. The howling wind and rain pelted them if they dared to raise their faces to look into the fury. Even the constant flashes of lightning did little to penetrate the darkness that surrounded them.

The Captain shouted something, and even though Michael was only inches away, the words were swallowed up by the storm and spit away into the maelstrom. Michael stared off into the void when the rains slackened for a brief moment, and the lightning flashes illuminated what lay ahead. Michael grabbed the wheel and began turning it furiously just as the ship's bow smashed into the jagged volcanic rocks.

Everyone on board was slammed into submission as the ship's hull was breached. With their forward motion now stopped, the overwhelming power of the sea pushed them sideways onto the rocks, and the ship flipped onto her side as her stout wooden beams and decking shrieked to the heavens as if for mercy. One of the ropes stretched across the deck snapped, and Michael watched as two of the crew dropped into the raging abyss below them. Michael looked over at the Captain, and their eyes met for a moment before they too were thrown into the blackness. Michael's last thought was of his beloved Katarina and their newborn child.

"BE NOT AFRAID OF GREATNESS, SOME ARE BORN GREAT, SOME ACHIEVE GREATNESS, AND SOME HAVE GREATNESS THRUST UPON THEM."

WILLIAM SHAKESPEARE, TWELFTH NIGHT ACT II SCENE 5

VENICE 1475
FILIPPI, SON OF MICHAEL, A
DESCENDANT OF RODNAN

The infant child was unusually strong and took to the wet nurse's breast easily. At the same time, his pleasant disposition allowed potential caregivers to seek him out from among the many unwanted squalling babies. Over his first seven years, the boy was often cared for by a mixture of women who all toiled along the waterfronts that catered to sailors from around the world. He was quiet but slightly large for his age, and his shock of red hair made him stand out even more.

He was sold along with two other boys his age to an innkeeper who took them to Florence's cosmopolitan city. The city teemed with merchants, artisans, craftsmen, guilds, shopkeepers, and even boasted of a university. The city held many pageants, festivals, and musical plays, which brought a steady stream of guests to the inn. The boys worked sweeping floors, emptying chamber pots, hauling water, and undertaking any other task deemed too demeaning for the innkeeper or his wife. The young boy proved industrious and made friends with many travelers who told him of faraway places that sounded wondrous, and he silently made plans to leave when the opportunity first afforded.

Filippi was eleven and one-half years of age, although he could easily pass for sixteen when he slipped onto the back of a cart and headed off toward Milan. Milan had more than three times the population of Florence, and Filippi thought that meant he would have three times the opportunity to make his way in the world. He spent a couple of weeks wandering around the city, keeping his eyes open for any situation that might be to his advantage.

One morning as he was walking along, his stomach began growling after a man walked past while eating a sizeable aromatic meat pie. Filippi followed the man into a small courtyard where he saw several men standing by easels painting and drawing pictures of a horse who stood before them, munching on some hay.

Filippi slipped past them unnoticed and stopped dead in his tracks as he looked upon a heaping platter of fruits and cheeses that no one seemed to be paying attention to. He cautiously moved closer while trying not to attract the notice of anyone. He started to reach out his hand when a strong authoritarian voice called out, "You there boy, come here."

Filippi looked over at the man who stood leaning over a table piled high with books while writing in a notebook. With a stern look, he waved the boy to come closer. Filippi edged nearer, and the older man's features softened a bit as he asked quietly, "What have we here?"

The man reached out his right hand and grasped the boy under the chin, and tilted his head upward and to the right, "Hold steady right there, boy." Without removing his right hand, the man began sketching with his left hand while Filippi tried to see what the man was drawing. Without looking up, the man calmly added, "Eyes straight ahead, boy." Filippi's stomach growled loudly, and the old man laughed, "Go and get something to eat and then come back here, boy." Filippi turned as the man asked, "What's your name, boy?" "Filippi, sir." The man reached out his hand and placed it gently on the boy's shoulder, "I am Leonardo, and this is my studio; perhaps we will find some work for you to do."

Over the weeks, months, and years to come, Filippi got to work with and know the old man who was the famous Leonardo Da Vinci. As Leonardo came to know the young boy, perhaps he took a particular interest in him because he too had grown up as a bastard child. Indeed, his father never legitimized him even after becoming a successful and famous artist.

Leonardo had been born just west of Florence in the town of Vinci in 1452. At age twelve, he moved to Florence to begin an eight-year-long apprentice to an engineer and artist who quickly determined that the boy was talented far beyond his years. Later he would move to Milan, and nearly ten years later, young Filippi would wander into his studio.

Leonardo was tall, muscular, and handsome with long curly hair, a disarming warm smile, and a manner that made friends of nearly everyone he met. He was gentle to a fault and was also a vegetarian due to his love of animals. The artist favored rose-colored cloaks and gowns, purple stockings, and a pink satin cap and saw that his assistants, including Filippi, dressed accordingly. Leonardo was continually perusing one of the many books that he kept scattered throughout the studio.

Filippi found it often difficult to carry on a conversation with his master because the man's mind seemed unable to concentrate on just one thing at a time. He might start talking about one thing, and mid-sentence, he would pick up his notebook and begin drawing or making calculations for some mechanical device or other.

Filippi sometimes accompanied him on his walks, where they might spend hours watching the water flow past in a stream with Leonardo making copious notes on its motion, flow and speed as it meandered around objects blocking its path. He could sit for long periods watching birds in flight, making intricate drawings and sketches of their wings' operations. Dead animals would be peeled apart layer by layer as copious notes would be taken. If they passed by people who caught his artist's eye, he would often ask them to pose as he sketched their portrait.

Daily he would meet with engineers to discuss and deliberate over the intricacies of bridge design, the best strategy for castle turrets, or even battle armor. He drew plans for fanciful machines that only existed as yet in his mind or any other of a thousand things that crossed his inquiring mind.

Filippi frequently removed his clothing and posed as Leonardo sketched and made notations as other assistants made copious measurements. They noted the distance from hairline to brow, the inside of the eye to the tip of the nose, the ear to the corner of the mouth, the bottom of the lip to the end of the chin, the chin to the navel, the navel to the genitals, the elbow to the wrist, the hip to the knee and dozens and dozens of others. Leonardo did this with both young boys such as Filippi and aged men too. With lean, tall ones and short, squat ones, always taking notes, always sketching, always learning something about how to better represent the human form in sculpture or painting to make it seem to come alive on the flat surface.

Leonardo, Filippi, and two other assistants left the studio carrying satchels. As the master moved off ahead, the boy asked where they were heading, and the other two laughed and said, "Just you wait." Soon they arrived at a local hospital where they went around to the rear entrance before they went down steep, dark, damp stairs. An earthy smell soon was replaced by that of moldy bread and perhaps spilled sour wine as they lit lamps and began removing kits full of instruments from the bags they had carried.

Filippi noticed what appeared to be some object on a large table draped with a dark woolen blanket. The lamps were brought in closer, and the blanket was drawn back to reveal the naked body of an older woman. Her skin appeared waxy and grayish, although the skin seemed pulled back tight on her bones.

With a practiced hand, Leonardo stepped forward and began making an incision from the top of her nose to the hairline as Filippi gasped. Slight smiles appeared on the three faces now looking directly at him, and Leonardo simply said, "Steady." He then went back to his work, where he shortly had the skin removed entirely from the woman's face. At this time, he picked up his notebook and began sketching, as did one of the assistants while the other continued working away at the body.

Leonardo moved back and forth between the body and his notebook frequently as he detailed each nerve, tendon, and ligament of the face. Then they removed the old woman's heart from within her chest as Leonardo carefully made incisions. At the same time, he described the expected narrowing and hardening of the arteries' walls. He then described the various chambers and valves and their respective functions. Filippi had moved several paces backward, and Leonardo added, "Go outside and get some fresh air."

Filippi turned to go, stopped, and took a deep breath of the foul air, and then turned around and stepped back up to the body, "How can I assist?"

The next thing he knew, several hours had slipped past, and the decomposing body could help them no more, so they wrapped the body carefully and affectionately in fresh linens for her burial, and then they departed.

When Filippi arrived at the studio the following day, there was a flurry of activity as Leonardo was preparing for a pageant before the Milan court. There would be children soaring through the air in costumes that seemed to mimic the colors of the rainbow, thunderbolts would be flung from the heavens, and fairies and dragons would burst forth across the stage and over the audience. Amidst it all would be Leonardo at the center of the stage narrating the story while playing the lyre, a seven-stringed instrument of his design and manufacture.

Filippi spent all day learning to fold small sheets of the thinnest tissue paper into a variety of vaguely human and animal-like shapes. These were then hand-painted in unique colors so that they appeared to sparkle as they flittered through the air. A large dragon perhaps three feet tall was made in the same manner. In all, it took three days to prepare everything for the performance.

On the evening of the show, Filippi was a part of the crew offstage, pulling levers and ropes that sent actors rising through the air. He found himself hidden inside what appeared to be a large tree just to the rear of the stage. As Leonardo told the story of tiny fairy princes and princesses who fought to save their kingdom from a mighty dragon, Filippi began pumping a leather bellows with his foot. This sent a stream of air up from the floor and out over the audience. He then slowly placed the tissue paper creatures into the airstream, where they fluttered and flittered high into the air. At first, they came slowly, and then dozens of them filled the air to the audiences' delight. Finally, the great dragon was released, and the assemblage gasped at the sight before breaking into thunderous applause as the dragon exploded in a brilliant, multicolored flash.

It wasn't long after that performance that the Duke of Milan commissioned Leonardo to paint the wall in the dining hall of a small church and monastery in the heart of Milan. He would spend more than three years working on the painting of The Last Supper, depicting the moment just after Jesus had told his twelve apostles, "One of you will betray me."

Filippi helped mix the double layer of dried plaster used to cover the walls that were fifteen feet high and twenty-nine feet long. This was followed by a white lead layer and finally the master himself using oil and tempera paint.

It was widely hailed as a masterpiece upon its completion, and Leonardo's fame was forever assured. Within two years,

Leonardo moved his studio once again back to Florence, where he spent much of his time being feted by royalty and wealthy benefactors. Filippi grew bored and left the studio, spending the next months moving from job to job.

Filippi entered into the famed Michelangelo di Lodovico Buonarroti Simoni studio, Frustrated and seeking some stability and security. Michelangelo was now twenty-five and one of the most sought-after sculptors and painters of the day. Filippi had met Michelangelo on more than one occasion when he was with Leonardo, and the two rival artists had crossed paths. Michelangelo had always been dismissive of the older Leonardo, who had likewise been negative in any comments about the younger man's work. Michelangelo had been born in Caprese, Tuscany, and raised in Florence. His mother died when he was but six, and after this, he had lived with a stonecutter whose home was near a quarry, and the young boys' talent for working with stone soon became evident. He was only thirteen when he was apprenticed to assist in painting the Sistine Chapel walls in Rome.

Filippi walked up to the celebrated man who was just three years older than himself and inquired about helping out in the studio. Michelangelo was walking in circles around a partially completed stone bust that sat atop a pedestal that could be itself turned; the robe he wore could have easily been mistaken for a rag as it was dusty and dirty and torn in several places. The man himself was coated in a fine layer of dust; he held a small chisel in his left hand and a slightly larger wooden mallet in his right. After some moments of silent contemplation, he set his tools down, turned to his visitor, and simply stated, "Fine, you can work here but stay out of my way."

Filippi soon found significant differences between his previous and current masters. Michelangelo rarely bathed and had to be reminded to eat. He was devout to his faith, pious and chaste, and quite often querulous and argumentative. He sought perfection in his work, and although he undertook many commissions for paintings, he did not consider himself a painter and referred to himself as a sculptor.

He was commissioned to carve a statue of Goliath's slayer from an imposing block of white marble that two other artists had turned down. He would spend the next two years working in near secrecy on his seventeen-foot tall sculpture of "David."

Called to Rome by Pope Julius II, Michelangelo was commissioned to paint the Sistine Chapel ceiling at the Vatican. Given virtual free reign over the project, he would spend the next four years on the undertaking. Michelangelo would do all of the actual finish painting himself. Filippi and the other assistants were kept busy with all of the preparatory work involving mixing and applying the layers of sand and lime used as the base and mixing the various paints. Michelangelo had to apply the paint while the base coat was still wet, which meant that the tasks must be repeated each day. Just building up the scaffold to reach the sixty-five-foot high ceiling was a feat in itself. The first time they could truly see the magnitude of the completed work was when the platform was finally removed at the end of the entire enterprise.

Michelangelo was rightfully feted for his magnificent works, and he would stay in Rome. Filippi decided that it was time for a change in his life, and he traveled back to Venice, where he had been born. He went seeking knowledge about his mother or father or the circumstances surrounding his birth nearly twenty-five years earlier. Of course, he found no one there who could remember the unremarkable life or death of a young woman or her lover who sailed off never to return.

Filippi had been frugal with any monies he had received during his years working for the great artists, and now he was determined to put that money to use. He found a vacant shop near the port that was for rent, and he quickly opened a small shop selling a variety of hard to find items used by the artisans of the city. His business grew swiftly, and he settled into life as a comfortable, respected, and profitable shopkeeper. He used his business proceeds to care for Venice's orphaned children and give them hope for a better future. He spent the remainder of his life in the pursuit of those goals.

"MAN CANNOT DISCOVER NEW
OCEANS UNLESS HE HAS THE COURAGE
TO LOSE SIGHT OF THE SHORE."

ANDRE GIDE

CADIZ, SPAIN 1492
QUIN AND ADAN MACCORMAC, SONS OF FRANCISCO, DESCENDANTS OF BRYAN, DESCENDANTS OF NIALL

win brothers Quin and Adan rode side by side as the forces of Isabella I of Castile and Ferdinand II of Aragon continued their nearly decade long fight to drive the Moors from the Emirate of Granada. Each spring, they would march into battle campaigns that would last until fall, when they would once again retire for the winter months. When they weren't pursuing combat with the Moors, they took action against the Jews to drive them out of Spain or force their conversion to Catholicism.

The two men were mounted heavy cavalry knights and had grown tired of the constant conflict and systematic persecution of peoples who, it seemed to them, were not much different than themselves. The men dreamt of another way to find adventure. They sat around the campfire quietly contemplating the stars above their heads when fortune smiled upon them as a comrade rode over and joined them.

Ponce de Leon was also a soldier, and he too had been long involved in these campaigns of war and was also casting his eyes elsewhere for challenge and adventure. He told the brothers that he was leaving soon for the port city of Cadiz, where he was hoping to join in a grand voyage of exploration to the new world in America and perhaps even on to exotic China. Their eyes lit up as they jumped to their feet, volunteering to join in this grand conquest.

Christopher Columbus had sailed to the new world with three ships and established settlements; upon his return, he was rapidly refitted for a second journey. This time he would lead a fleet of seventeen ships and more than twelve hundred men, several friars, some two hundred private investors, and a small cavalry troop of which Quin and Adan were among. The ships also held livestock, sheep, cattle, and horses for the use of the settlers in establishing permanent colonies in the name of Spain.

In September of 1493, just six months after returning from his first voyage of discovery, Columbus led his fleet back to sea, heading to Hispaniola and the West Indies. The island they saw first he named Dominica. Heading north, they named several more islands, including Montserrat, Antigua, Redondo, Nevis, Saint Kitts, Saint Martin, Saint Croix, and others, including the Virgin Islands. They landed at Puerto Rico and then Hispaniola, where Columbus had left a fort and a contingent of forty men tasked with beginning the settlement of this land.

In Hispaniola, they found the fort destroyed and the men gone, with only a few unmarked graves to note their passing. Ponce de Leon would stay here in what would become Santo Domingo as the settlers staked their claims to the land and began the arduous tasks of cultivating crops and building shelters. Quin and Adan stayed together, excited at the prospect of being pioneers and landowners themselves. Columbus would sail away with three ships looking for mainland China which he believed was nearby.

Farming proved difficult at best, and many quickly grew tired from their efforts. When word first spread of gold being found,

many of the men deserted their fledgling farms, abandoning them back to the tropical forest as they went off in search of the ever-elusive treasure.

Columbus would eventually sail back to Spain, while de Leon would stay behind as a provincial Governor. After hearing of gold on nearby Puerto Rico, he gathered his troops, including his cavalry, with Quin and Adan and sailed there. They would conquer the island in bloody fighting while giving no quarter to the natives there, and soon the island was claimed in honor of Spain, and Ponce de Leon was named its Governor. He would remain as Governor until 1511 when he would be removed from that office due to his cruelty and brutality to the indigenous peoples and be replaced by Diego Columbus, Christopher's Son.

Adan would return to Spain, marry his sweetheart, and together they would sail back to Hispaniola, where they would join in a now-thriving colony in Santo Domingo. Quin had fallen for a dark-skinned island girl and soon had a growing family of his own, finding peace and solace for the first time in his life.

Ponce de Leon had long heard tales from the natives of a mythical place in the lands to the north where the waters had miraculous healing powers, and those who bathed and drank from them lived long and healthful lives. They were even stories of the aged who grew not older but returned to the vim and vigor of their youth via the phenomenon of these wondrous waters.

He led expeditions to Bimini, the Bahamas, and to new lands that they reached on Palm Sunday. He named the land Pascua de Florida or a place of flowers and claimed it for Spain. Their exhaustive search could find no sign of healing waters or the mysterious fountain of youth, and the natives in the area proved to be unfriendly towards their intrusion.

Ponce de Leon would return to Spain amid great acclamation, and the King proclaimed him a Captain-General. A few years later, he would again plan a return to Florida in search of the curative powers of the mystical waters. Adan would leave his wife and family, and along with two hundred other men, they would join de Leon on this mission that ventured up the west coast of Florida. Quin was out on a lengthy expedition searching for gold in the mountains and unable to return in time to join in on this latest expedition.

Ponce de Leon stepped off the boat with Adan at his side, and they moved toward the thick line of trees and high grasses that lined the shore. Here they were met by a volley of arrows from the warriors of the native tribes. Several men went down immediately, including both Ponce and Adan. The men were helped back to their boats as they fended off the attack. They fled from the shores of Florida and headed back out to sea. They made landfall in Havana, Cuba, and Ponce de Leon was taken ashore, where he would later die from his wound in July of 1521.

Adan had been wounded in the left shoulder, and although it became infected and he suffered a high fever for more than a fortnight, he did survive to return to his family. Upon his recovery, he made a solemn vow to his wife that his days of searching for adventure were over and that he would remain by her side forevermore.

"COURAGE IS NOT THE ABSENCE OF FEAR, BUT RATHER THE JUDGMENT THAT SOMETHING ELSE IS MORE IMPORTANT THAN FEAR."

AMBROSE REDMOON

PORTUGAL 1519
MIGUEL JUAN MACCORMAC, SON OF FRANSISCO, A DESCENDANT OF BRYAN, A DESCENDANT OF NIALL

Miguel MacCormac was a fifth-generation mariner and cartographer or map-maker. He was one of seven brothers whose lives revolved around ships and the sea. His grandfather had sailed with legendary Spanish explorer Henry the Navigator on many of his daring voyages of exploration along the African coast. Prince Henry of Portugal had also been governor of the Order of Christ from 1420 until he died in 1460, and many members of the order naturally followed his lead to become rulers of the country.

Miguel had planned to sail with Vasco De Gama in 1497 on a journey around the Cape of Africa and on to India. Fortune had not smiled upon him as he took ill with fever shortly before the fleet was to sail. It would be another seven years, and now Miguel was twenty-five years of age before he would sail with a fleet of ships to India on a journey that would last almost eight years. During this time, he developed an unlikely friendship with a boy named Ferdinand, who had been noble-born and wealthy and who by the age of ten had been a page for the Portuguese Queen Leonor.

Ferdinand Magellan was also twenty-five when the fleet had set sail. Upon completion of the voyage nearly a decade later, Magellan had fallen out of favor with the Portuguese, and he would eventually leave for Spain.

The Spanish crown had commissioned expeditions hoping to discover routes to the west. In 1513 Vasco Nunez de Balboa had reached the Pacific Ocean after crossing the Isthmus of Panama while others were dying while exploring South America. During these exciting times, Magellan proposed a bold expedition to the Spanish King, Charles I, the future Holy Roman Emperor Charles V.

The king gave Magellan a fleet of five ships and a crew of two hundred and seventy men from many different nations. Miguel gladly accepted the offer to sail with his old friend Magellan once again, and in August of 1519, they set sail from Seville.

The expedition sailed first to Cape Verde off Africa's coast before setting course across the Atlantic for Brazil. They avoided landing in Brazil as this was Portuguese territory; instead, they moved south along the coastline before dropping anchor in Rio De Janeiro. From here, the ships again sailed south, looking for the strait that Magellan thought would lead them to the Spice Islands.

They established a settlement to spend the winter, and on Easter morning, a mutiny occurred. Three of his five captains were involved. Two were almost immediately captured and executed by being drawn and quartered, and their remains staked out on the beach as a deterrent to any further similar actions. The third captain was left marooned on a remote stretch of the coast.

Later one of the ships was lost in a wreck, although the crew was rescued. By October, the four remaining vessels found a passage to the Pacific in what would come to be known as the

Strait of Magellan. He sent one ship off to explore the route, but the commander deserted, and the ship instead sailed back to Spain. Magellan led his three remaining ships through until they reached the ocean he named Pacifico due to its stillness.

Miguel stood at Magellan's side as they sailed northwest until they reached the Marianas Islands and Guam. By March, they made it to the Philippines with only one hundred and fifty remaining crew members

Magellan had, on his voyage in 1511, taken on a Malaysian man as his indentured servant. He had named the man Enrique, and he would now serve a vital role as an interpreter with the native tribes. The Rajah of Cebu was friendly to Magellan and the Spaniards as he and his Queen had been baptized as Christians. The Rajah convinced Magellan to attack and kill his enemy DataLapuLapu on the nearby smaller island of Mactan.

Magellan sent Miguel and Enrique to Mactan, attempting to convert LapuLapu to Christianity but, the offer was dismissed at spear point. On April 27, 1521, Magellan sailed to Mactan with just half of his forces. Fifty men led by Magellan and Miguel waded ashore armed with muskets and crossbows. Here they were met by an opposing party of fifteen hundred warriors. The muskets and crossbows fired unceasingly for nearly half an hour until they could no longer hold back the oncoming tribesmen.

Ferdinand Magellan and Miguel MacCormac stood shoulder to shoulder as their troops waded back to the boats. A bamboo spear impaled in Magellan's shoulder as he took one native down with his lance. Miguel furiously swung his sword until both he and his captain were cut down and killed.

As a result of the loss of so many men in the fighting, the expedition did not have enough men to sail all three ships, and one was abandoned and burned. The two ships would sail west until reaching the Spice Islands of Maluku. The fully laden ships set sail for Spain weeks later, but one of them began taking on water, and attempts to repair it were unsuccessful. The smaller of the ships could not hold all of the remaining crew and set sail for home. The damaged ship endeavored to return but was captured by the Portuguese and later wrecked in a storm while at anchor.

The lone remaining ship, the Victoria, rounded the Cape of Good Hope on May 6, having exhausted its food supplies, and twenty crewmen would die of starvation before they could make port. More of the crew was abandoned before the ship made its final push on its three-year journey home as the first ship to have circumnavigated the world. Only eighteen survivors of the voyage walked off the Victoria in Seville harbor in 1522.

"I CAME, I SAW, I CONQUERED."

JULIUS CAESAR

SPAIN 1530

ROBERTO AND HERNANDO MACCORMAC, SONS OF LUIS MACCORMAC, DESCENDANTS OF RONAN

As tales of Hernan Cortes' exploits and his conquistadors' conquest of the Aztec empire filled their heads, the brothers Roberto and Hernando MacCormac joined Francisco Pizarro sailing from Seville, Spain, heading to Central and South America. In January of the year, 1530 after first landing in Panama, the Spaniards would be reinforced with men under the command of another explorer and conquistador, Hernando De Soto. Pizarro led men searching for a treasure that now lay in the hands of an empire known as the Inca.

The Inca tribes had, at the height of their civilization, numbered nearly ten million people with untold wealth in the manner of precious stones, gold, and silver. The Inca prized these items as purely ornamental and gave them little value. They had no written language, and the spoken word was used throughout their vast lands. A system of roads was built and maintained; one, particularly, stretched nearly one thousand miles and reached thirty feet wide in many places. Houses were built every seven miles along its length, and runners moved between these houses carrying oral messages from even the most remote areas of the empire.

Huayna Capac had led the Inca people for many years when a smallpox epidemic had swept through Mexico and down through Central America until it had finally reached Peru and the Incas. A quarter of a million of his people died before he too, succumbed to its ravages. His death led to a five-year civil war between his two sons Huascar and Atahualpa, as they and their armies fought for control. Millions died as entire cities were destroyed and their citizens slaughtered. Atahualpa's warriors eventually captured Huascar, and he was executed.

Into this landscape, Pizarro led his men in search of fame and fortune. He split his forces in two, with his pilot Bartolome Ruiz taking command of half the men, including the brothers MacCormac. Roberto and Hernando were scouting ahead in a small boat when they came across a large balsa raft carrying a massive sail made of cotton.

Aboard the craft were twenty Inca tribesmen. Roberto and Hernando were welcomed and amazed by the amount of gold, silver, emeralds, and diamonds that adorned all the Incas. Many delicate fabrics were interwoven with all of these and other precious stones. Roberto was offered a small disc of gold, which he placed in his mouth and bit down to test its density. At this, the Incas burst into fits of laughter at the sight of the strange white-skinned men with hair on their faces who would eat gold.

The brothers MacCormac were sent as emissaries to seek out the Incan leader Atahualpa, and after an arduous and treacherous journey, they arrived at the city of Caxamalca. In the days that followed, the one hundred and sixty Spaniards set up camp in a walled-in courtyard area surrounded by some fifty thousand men of the Inca army. The Spanish were armed with crossbows and early guns known as a harquebus. They also had sixty horse-mounted cavalry. The horse was unknown to the Inca, and they were both terrified and awed by them.

Atahualpa accepted an invitation to meet with the Spaniards, and nearly one thousand of his courtiers joined him in their finest ceremonial garments. Once they were all inside the Spaniard's camp, Atahualpa was seized while all others were savagely and brutally slaughtered before his eyes. The Incan army that surrounded them was unsure what to do and eventually fled back into the forests.

Atahualpa was for months held prisoner in a room seventeen feet wide by twenty-two feet long. When he realized the Spanish lust for gold and silver, he offered to fill the space from bottom to top with gold and twice over with silver in return for his release.

A long line of Incan people carried intricately hand-woven baskets filled with the prized gold and silver to the Spaniards to fulfill the bargain. Still, they had Atahualpa executed as the conquistadores sought to subdue control over the entire empire. All of the precious metal was melted down into ingots and bars to be shipped back to Spain.

Roberto contracted malaria during this time and died from the resulting high fever. A broken-hearted Hernando sailed back to Spain along with one of the shipments of Incan treasure. The ship carrying their immeasurably valuable bounty sailed off into clear skies and calm seas that turned dark and violent two days later. She went down in the storm with the loss of the entire crew and its precious cargo.

"SET OUT FROM ANY POINT. THEY
ARE ALL ALIKE. THEY ALL LEAD
TO A POINT OF DEPARTURE."

ANTONIO PORCHIA

COUNTY OF WEXFORD IN THE SOUTHEAST OF IRELAND 1645
DINISH MACCORMAC, SON OF WILLEM, A DESCENDANT OF RODNAN

inish was just sixteen years of age when he wed the fifteen-year-old Laura, and within a year, she would give birth to a male child that would only live for two days. A year later, she again lost a child in the birthing process. A strong son named John brought relief and joy into their lives just two years later. The following year Laura would again be with child when fever took her and her unborn to the grave.

Dinish struggled as a tenant farmer, and after three successive years of poor crops, he found himself thrown off the land by his landlord. With no real prospects and nearing starvation, he took the only option he felt that he had. He offered his son up for indentured servitude in the New World of America in return for a small sum of money and his son's passage on a ship going to a better life.

Seven-year-old John stood wide-eyed, watching with excitement at the whirlwind of activities that pulsed before him. Dinish held his son's hand as he stood stoically by. John had only a small woolen sack holding his meager few possessions, the most precious of which was a piece of parchment containing a long curly lock of his mother's hair.

The commotion occurring as the sailing ship Jennie Lynn was loaded with all manner of goods and supplies captivated the young boy who could not understand why his father looked so forlorn. Finally, after all of the valuable goods were on board, a call was made for the human cargo to step forward as their names were called.

Dinish took his son's chin in his hand and tilted the boy's face upward.

"You will have to be strong lad,"

"I will, father," replied the eager boy.

With a strong will and hiding a broken heart, Dinish added, "I will not be able to join you on this journey."

Just then, his name was called, and as he cried, his father took his sack and led him up to the gangplank. A long hug and a short kiss on the cheek were all that time allowed as the boy was pulled onto the ship that would be his home for the next fifty-five days.

The boy and twenty-six other passengers, mostly children under ten, were crammed below decks into two cargo holds alongside various farm animals. The stench was nearly unbearable within the closed quarters. John preferred to huddle on deck whenever possible, where at least the wind and splash of the sea brought a measure of relief from the odors below. It took several days for his stomach to become accustomed to the swaying motion of the ship, and only then was he able to keep down any portion of his once-daily ration of hard biscuit.

After picking out the maggots and weevils, the biscuit was mashed, and water added until the soggy mixture became somewhat edible. Once a week, each of them was given a small ration of what passed as meat, and John was usually able to stretch it out to last for four or five days. Sometimes he shared his ration with a small girl named Katherine who hung onto his shirt as if her very life depended upon it. Fear showed in the five-year-old girl's eyes at all times except for when she felt the protective embrace of John.

Six or seven of the children huddled below in a tangled mass as a storm raged outside. They had become used to the ship's creaks and moans, but now the vessel seemed to be crying out in mortal pain as it was battered from all sides. Mumbled prayers could be heard above the howling winds and the crashing waves that attacked the ship. Katherine buried her face into John's chest and hugged him as tightly as her tiny arms would allow.

An older girl named Anne, who had been sickly the entire voyage, lay across Johns' legs wrapped up in a desperate embrace with two other children. Ropes had been interwoven across the holds, and everyone who could, held tight lest they find themselves thrown about as the ship twisted and turned her way through the storm.

The hatch above opened, and amid the howl of the tempest and the inrushing sea came two crew members seeking some refuge from the elements. They tumbled down into the mass of children below as cries and screams erupted. One crewman was thrown sideways and crashed into a massive timber that was part of the ship's structure. Blood splattered, and he was split open from the top of his head down to the jawline. At first, his body went limp, and then he lay next to the children twitching for a minute or two before again falling still. The terrified children stared at the lifeless body until John tossed a piece of canvas over him.

John awoke to find that the storm had, at last, spit them from its fury, and the seas were once again calm. The girl Anne was now being wrapped up in a tattered blanket. She lay in a row with four others, including the crewmen who had died at their feet. All were taken up on deck, and the captain spoke solemnly before each was lifted over the side and dropped into the vastness of the ocean. John looked down at Katherine, who stared silently at the proceedings; her face was a blank slate that he could not read.

In the weeks that followed, the meager meat rations ran out, and three more children and two of the crew fell victim to starvation and became one with the sea. John felt a numbing pain throughout his body as he stared out at the endless waters in desperation.

"Land Ho!"

The call brought renewed life to all aboard, and tears of relief streamed down the cheeks of all remaining souls aboard the battered vessel.

At anchor, they watched as two boats rowed out to them, bringing life-sustaining water and food. They would not be allowed off the ship until a doctor had inspected them all. Although finally given fresh water and twice-daily rations of food, they would have to remain in quarantine for another ten days before they could once more step upon ground that did not sway beneath their feet.

"IT IS DANGEROUS TO BE RIGHT
IN MATTERS WHERE ESTABLISHED
MEN ARE WRONG."

———————

VOLTAIRE

CHESAPEAKE BAY, VIRGINIA 1655

JOHN MACCORMAC, SON OF DINISH, GRANDSON OF WILLEM, A DESCENDANT OF RODNAN

One by one, the passengers' names were called, and they were taken into a small tent to find out their fate. Katherine dug her face into John's side as her name rang out, and she had to be pried from his grasp. The five-year-old was taken into the tent as John asked one of the men holding papers in his hand, "Where's she going."

The man looked down on the boy and scratched at his scraggly beard, "None of your business but, she will become a settler's wife. He paid for her voyage over and will rightly claim her now."

A few minutes later, the voice called out hesitantly as the man squinted at the smeared ink on the passenger manifest, "John Carmack." The name was called out a second time, and John was shoved forward by the bearded man.

As John stepped into the tent, he saw two men seated at

a small table and one tall, taciturn man with a flowing white beard standing to the side. One of the seated men motioned him forward as the man beside him spoke, "John Carmack, age nine, you will be obligated..."

John spoke up, "I am only seven, and my name is..."

"Quiet," the man shouted. "You now belong to Mr. Andrew Portman for the next seven years or until you reach the age of sixteen." The man nodded to Mr. Portman, "He is now yours, sir."

Mr. Portman stepped up to the table and signed some papers before turning to John, "Come boy." He then turned and walked out of the rear of the tent, and John quickly followed. His new master climbed up on an old nag of a horse and began riding off. John broke into a trot to keep up.

Thirty minutes later, John stopped and stared as a large group of strange people passed in the opposite direction. Their brown skin was mostly exposed; they wore animal skins and had feathers tucked into their hair. Johns' mouth gaped open as he looked upon these members of the Algonquin Indian tribe. It was not until his new master swatted him with his horsewhip that the spell was broken.

Upon arriving at what was to be his new home, he was in for yet another shock as he looked upon the many black-skinned people who stared at him with blank expressions. The master spoke to one of the black women as she looked down at the boy with a disapproving gaze. She took John by the hand and led him into a small shack.

"Here child, this will be your new home." He tried to explain that they had his name and age both wrong. The stern-faced woman shook a gnarled bony finger at him and admonished him, "You'll answer to whatever Master calls you, or you'll get the whip boy."

John found that the Negroes were slaves of the master and that he was also thought of as a slave, although perhaps set a step above them due to his skin color. At first, he was mostly ignored by the others until they saw that he was treated as poorly as they were, and gradually he blended in with them as just another piece of property. It wasn't until two years later that he was allowed to sleep in the master's house along with a couple of the other house slaves.

Four more years went by quickly as John learned that Andrew Portman was a stern master who rarely spared the rod or the lash whenever his mood darkened, and that seemed to happen daily. After a severe beating for not responding fast enough to a command, John ran off as soon as darkness fell. He was apprehended three days later, and after another whipping, he was informed that his indentured servitude was to be extended by another two years due to his running off.

During the following winter, Mr. Portman became ill and remained confined to bed, lingering until spring before succumbing to his illness. John found life better under the service of the Portman children but still relished the thought of earning his freedom and beginning life on his own, even as he had no idea where he would go or what he might do. He just knew that he would finally be on his own.

On an October day in 1664, John was called into the front room by Master Portman. The latter unceremoniously handed him a paper that noted that he was no longer indebted to the Portman family and was hereby a free man. As per the custom of the day, he was given a new set of clothes referred to as his freedom clothes and sent on his way. John was now 16 years of age as he made his goodbyes to the other slaves whose only liberty from slavery would come upon their death. Their ancestors would have to wait another two-hundred years for their ultimate emancipation.

"ANYTHING YOU CAN IMAGINE,
YOU CAN MAKE REAL."

JULES VERNE

VIRGINIA WILDERNESS 1664
JOHN CARMACK, SON OF DINISH, GRANDSON OF WILLEM, A DESCENDANT OF RODNAN

John walked for days wide-eyed into the unknown future with youthful exuberance in his step. One afternoon he snared a rabbit and cooked it beside a stream near a dense thicket of brush at the foot of seemingly impenetrable mountains. Just after beginning his meal, he watched as a solitary figure walked toward him, leading three pack mules laden down with all manner of gear and supplies. The smiling man stopped a few feet away from the fire and knelt on one knee.

"That rabbit smells real nice. Is it big enough for two?"

John smiled back at the seemingly friendly stranger, "I reckon so."

The man stretched out his hand, "Amos Josiah Waters."

"John Carmack."

Amos took a bite from the rabbit and spoke as he chewed, "So what's a young man such as yourself doing out here on the far edge of civilization? You don't seem to have much in the way of gear."

John stood with his chin up, and his head held high. "I recently was released from the service of the Portman family, and I have heard tell of wilderness areas where land can be bought on credit as long as you agree to clear it and work it. That's what I aim to do, sir."

Amos rose to his full height, and stared hard at the young man in silence, looked up into the mountains while scratching at his beard, "You have any weapons, son?"

John's puzzled expression warranted Amos to expand upon his question, "A rifle, do you have a rifle?"

John defiantly held up a small knife as he answered, "I can trap; I was able to feed you supper, wasn't I?"

Amos burst into laughter, "Yes indeed, cept that knife a'yorn ain't going to scare off no bear now is it? Nor Indians neither." Amos smiled, "Don't suppose you got an ax now, do ya?"

John looked over at the mule, "Bet you got all that and more."

With a chuckle, Amos continued, "I believe I am better supplied than you, my young friend."

The older man pointed towards the hills in the distance, "You know them mountains?"

John scowled, "You sure got a lot a questions."

Amos shot back, "You sure don't have many answers. Those are the Appalachian Mountains and over to the Blue Ridge and then another wide ocean called the Pacific."

John's jaw dropped wide open as he remembered the long voyage he had undertaken as a young boy, "An ocean over those mountains? As big as the Atlantic?"

Amos shook his head slowly, "Don't nobody rightly know, just yet. Maybe we could find out if you're interested."

John stepped forward, "Why yes sir."

The two men shook hands as each dreamt of the adventures yet to come.

In the weeks to come, the two new friends moved deeper into the forests heading westward into dangerous territory where few if any settlers had been before. They sat in council with various Indian tribes, which allowed them to pass peacefully.

It was a chieftain with the Monacan tribe, a Siouxian people who spoke in the Algonquian language, who agreed to send six of his warriors and guides to lead them through the mountains beyond the Blue Ridge toward sacred hunting grounds. While they went out on this scouting mission, John and Amos would leave a good portion of their supplies with the chief whose people were dying from a strange illness that Amos thought was influenza. They would also travel by river along the waters called Kanawha.

Ten days later, they reached an area of the river that the natives had never before seen and had only heard stories by elders who told of wild, raging waters that could not be ridden or tamed. The roar of the water echoed off the rock faces as they paddled onward. The eight men were divided between four canoes. John rode with one Monacan warrior who rarely spoke. Amos also shared a canoe with the leader of the group, who was a son of the tribal chief. Each of the other canoes held a pair of young tribesmen who were often far ahead scouting for danger. These men would usually not be seen for hours until they had already made camp and were sitting happily eating either fish or game around the fire.

The four canoes drifted in the relatively calm waters near the river's edge while they decided whether to proceed through the turbulent and rough water ahead. The ordinarily fearless scouts showed signs of apprehension about moving forward. As they sat contemplating portaging around this section of the river, the decision was made for them as a volley of arrows sliced through the air.

One scout from each of the lead canoes was hit and toppled into the waters as the other tribesmen grabbed their bows and searched for targets among the dense tree line just back from the river's rocky edge. Amos fired his rifle and John his pistol as more arrows rained down upon them, and they had no choice but to paddle out into the faster current in the center of the river.

John took one last look over his shoulder at more than thirty Iroquois who jeered and shouted at their departure. He now thought them lucky to have escaped. John was jolted back to the task at hand as the rough water splashed over him in a torrential spray. There was no time for thought, only to react and perhaps to pray for salvation from the hellish forces at work on the river.

Coming out of one particularly rough patch, John was able to catch a glimpse of only one other canoe but could not tell if anyone was still in the craft or not before the fury of the monstrous river again devoured them.

The canoe spun sideways and then crashed heavily into a series of massive boulders before John found himself flung into the raging waters and pulled underneath the roiling waters. He tumbled head over heels as he thrashed his arms about for something to hold onto until he lost any sense of up or down or left or right.

Amos was faring only slightly better as he was able to maintain a grasp on the side of his canoe after being thrown clear of a jagged outcropping of rock that nearly broke the craft in two. As he held on for dear life, the side of his ankle cracked into a submerged rock that shredded his flesh and shattered his bones.

John lay on the shoreline gasping for breath for several minutes before he could even raise his head to look around for the others. Finally making it to his feet, he stood doubled over with his hands on his knees before heading downstream.

Around the next bend, he spotted a figure moving on the opposite shore. His hopes that his partner had survived soared as he saw the chief's son who had been in the canoe with Amos. He yelled across and continued following the river's current. He soon found Amos unconscious amid the remains of his canoe.

Jagged edges of bone protruded through Amos's ankle's skin,

and his foot lay at an odd angle. The skin was swollen and discolored, and John knew it was likely to cost Amos his life.

John had once seen a slave named Andrew, who had stepped in a gopher hole and broken the bones in his ankle and shin. Master Portman had been furious and sent for the doctor who lived only half a day's ride away. The doctor examined the leg, spoke in whispers with the master, and then began wrapping a small length of rope around his leg below the knee.

John helped hold Andrew down as the doctor ran a file across the blade of an ax. John watched in horror as the blade fell, and Andrew screamed. Despite the attempt at removing the damaged limb, Andrew became fevered and died ten days later. Master Portman whipped the dead body as a warning to the others to be more careful with his property.

John wrapped Amos up as best he could and built a small fire to help dry him out. The chiefs' son had made his way across the river, collecting up one of the young scouts as they were the only other survivors. After they looked at the broken leg, the scout sat on Amos's thigh and grabbed tightly to his knee while his stone-faced chief took hold of the foot and yanked sharply downward.

Amos let out a grunt amid the crunching sound of the bone mashing back together. They wrapped some rawhide strapping tightly around the injured ankle and then sat back in silence.

After a meal of fresh fish had satisfied them, John sat by the fire watching Amos while their guides quietly disappeared into the woods. Amos spent the following two days, drifting into and out of consciousness before sitting up straight, smiling brightly, and in a soft, pleasant voice called out, "Mama." Amos then toppled over, never to awaken.

John slid his partners' body out into the current and watched as it was washed away. For another three days, he paced around the camp, wondering if he should try to make his way back or stay and wait for the guides who might never return. He decided to give them one more night and leave in the morning.

With no sign of them at daylight, John began walking back upstream along the river. Much of the river was bordered by high rock cliffs and nearly impenetrable forest, making the return trip much more difficult.

Five days into his journey John nearly ran into an Iroquois hunting party numbering close to ten warriors. He had to hide from them as they were possibly still searching for him after the attack on the river that had cost him his short-lived friendship with Amos. Giving them a wide berth added more time to his travels, but it seemed a wise alternative to attempting to slip past them.

John awoke to see the young scout sitting cross-legged in front of the fire smiling at him. Somehow they had tracked him for over a week through the forest while also avoiding the Iroquois. The chiefs' son appeared from the thick brush holding a large rabbit, and they enjoyed a morning meal before heading off toward the Monacan camp a mere four days away.

In camp, John claimed the remainder of the supplies they had left behind. He shared some things with the tribe members, made his goodbyes, and headed back east toward what he hoped were lands that he could claim as his own and make his stake in the world.

Upon finally reaching Fort Henry, he was indeed able to purchase land that would genuinely become his only after working the land for five years and building a homestead upon it.

IRELAND 1667
DINISH MACCORMAC, SON OF WILLEM, A DESCENDANT OF RODNAN

inish MacCormac used the money he had received from his son's indentured servitude, bought a small boat, and took to the sea, fishing in the rough coastal waters. His fortunes ebbed and flowed like the sea tides, and after a series of poor excursions, his debts amounted to more than his meager assets, and his boat was taken from him.

His protests to the English magistrate appointed by Oliver Cromwell to handle local disputes went unheeded. Dinish soon found himself one of the many destitute and penniless souls in the streets. Rounded up by the English, he was placed in shackles and imprisoned.

After languishing in a cramped and overcrowded cell for several months, he and the other impoverished souls found themselves loaded onto ships under cover of darkness. They knew not where they were headed, having heard only rumors of ships going to Africa, the East Indies, and the New World. Dinish dreamt of reuniting with his son John and forging a new life together in these new lands.

The first night Dinish lay chained alongside eighty-one men, of whom he knew only a handful. They lie side by side and head to foot in their filth and excrement.

Nearly two months and thirty-five hundred nautical miles later, Dinish lay fevered and trembling alongside the other surviving souls who now numbered forty-two. Dinish was unconscious when the ship made landfall.

ISLAND OF BARBADOS 1667
DINISH MACCORMAC, SON OF WILLEM,
A DESCENDANT OF RODNAN

inish had to be carried off the ship due to his weakened state. He asked one of the dockworkers where they were. The man spoke in Portuguese, and Dinish struggled to understand him. The man stroked his fingers along his cheeks and chin as a sailor interpreted for him. "The island is called Barbados. In Portuguese, it means Bearded One, named for the fig trees with their long hanging roots that resemble a beard."

Dinish soon found himself working in the sugar cane fields of one of the many plantations on Barbados. Having been expelled from Ireland, he was now forced to live as an indentured servant for the next seven years. Although his treatment was poor, it was still a step ahead of the brutality endured by the African slaves brought in by the hundreds.

Dinish spent his seven years dreaming only of his son John, who was alone in America's colonies. Fantasies of one day reuniting with his son drove him through the oppressive heat of the Caribbean sun, the pain inflicted by his masters, through the long days, and the loneliness of many sleepless nights.

He voluntarily undertook extra work whenever possible to occasionally earn a little something extra from guards or the overseers. Everything was squirreled away in hopes of gaining passage once his freedom was secured.

At long last, his freedom from servitude came in the year 1674, and he stood tall and for a time did not feel the weight of his forty-five years of age.

He headed straight to the docks seeking work, where he eventually made friends with a native of Barbados, a man of Scottish descent named William Woodward, who gave him work. After several months he was able to earn passage aboard a privateer hauling goods to the colonies.

"WHEN THE SUN HAS SET, NO
CANDLE CAN REPLACE IT."

GEORGE R.R. MARTIN

FORT HENRY – THE VIRGINIA TERRITORY 1668

JOHN CARMACK, SON OF DINISH, GRANDSON OF WILLEM, A DESCENDANT OF RODNAN MACCORMAC

John had indeed claimed a parcel of land near Fort Henry as his own and built a homestead upon it. He had met a young woman named Mary Clarke and, within weeks, became her husband. In the next ten years, they had six children, four boys and two girls. He was living what he could only believe was a dream from his dire beginnings in Ireland.

In 1684 a cholera epidemic swept throughout the colonies devastating both the native Indian population and the settlers who fought to survive in the wilderness areas. Mary and their two youngest sons all succumbed to the scourge.

John forged onward, claiming more land and cultivating the crops that would sustain them. Then he lost another son to snakebite while playing in a stream within a short distance from their home.

John's grief was evident to his remaining son and two

daughters. His eldest son Nathaniel and oldest daughter Emmaline were inseparable, often hunting together in the forests near their home. Both were accomplished with a bow or musket, often coming home with provisions that kept the family fed as their father stayed close to the fields and their home.

Nathaniel and Emmaline went out hunting one day and chose to venture farther from their home than ever before, searching for game to fill their family larder. As they moved deeper into the dense forest Emmy raced on ahead of her brother, laughing as she played and daring him to keep up.

He caught a glimpse of her just as she disappeared into a thicket of brush and rushed to catch up. He came to a small stream near a hillside and wondered where she might be hiding when he spied her kneeling farther up and on the opposite side of the creek.

She held up a hand to her ear and motioned to him. He froze in his tracks and listened intently but heard nothing. She scampered up the creek bed and was lost in the brush.

He pushed on, barely squeezing through to find his sister on her hands and knees. Dropping down beside her, he whispered, "What did you hear? A war party?"

She giggled, "Listen, silly."

A low whistling sound came out of the hillside.

"A cave," she exclaimed with excitement. Before he could comment, she rushed forward toward a darkened spot almost hidden by dense shrubs.

Nathaniel rushed to her side. He pushed her aside and climbed through the narrow opening as she called out, "No fair, I found it first."

Crawling through the darkness for some twenty feet, they came to an opening almost big enough to stand up in. Here they used a flint to make a small fire that they, in turn, used to make two torches to explore their find.

Deeper they went into the tunnel, overwhelmed with

excitement at what treasures they might find. Twenty minutes later, they came into a larger open chamber with a steep slope covered in perfectly round rocks and stones. They slid down until they reached the bottom and neared a dark spot they believed to be yet another tunnel.

Emmaline said, "I want to go first this time."

Before Nathaniel could respond, some of the rocks on the slope began tumbling down upon them. They could not see their peril in the flickering torchlight, and soon the rocks covered their feet and ankles. Nathaniel dropped his torch as he desperately tried to free himself. Emmaline cried out as a stone hit her square in the back.

The rocks continued cascading down upon them, and soon they were buried waist-deep. Nathaniel reached his hand back and grabbed Emmaline, "Em, I'm trapped."

"Me too," she answered.

As the rocks continued piling up around them, Nathaniel called out, "I'm sorry Em, I love you."

He never heard her reply as they were buried under the avalanche of stone.

John sat in eerie silence as he ate dinner with his youngest daughter Madeline. He knew the skills of his two oldest children and tried not to worry as night fell. By morning he paced outside their cabin, watching for them while trying to push away the sense of dread that crept over him.

By midday, he had sent Maddy off to Fort Henry as he ventured out after his children. His first stop was to the Monacan village, where he was well known as a friend. Inquiries about his children brought several elders to send out a search party.

Parties from Fort Henry also searched for several days to no avail. It was then that John packed Maddy off to stay with friends so that he could go out and find his children now feared captured by unfriendly tribal war parties.

For days on end, he searched, stopping at every Indian village he came across. His fearlessness kept him safe as he asked for information about his children. Many times he was offered help in his search but, he moved on alone in his quest.

The weeks turned into months as he moved into lands, where few if any white men had ever ventured. Hearing tales of white children being taken north, he moved in that direction heading along the Ohio River valley.

He made it to Niagara's falls but had no interest in the great falls, moving past them without noticing their power and beauty. He moved west along the lake called Erie before hearing from French trappers of white children taken south.

The next month's found him heading in that direction by raft and canoe, sometimes traveling with various tribes or fur trappers but, most often alone. As the seasons passed, he moved ever southward in his search.

John reached New Orleans in the summer of 1688 while reeling from malaria and its accompanying fever. He stopped anyone who would speak to this wild apparition from the wilderness and asked about his children. A family took him in and allowed him to rest for several weeks before he regained enough strength to resume his quest.

Months later, he returned to his home to find the farmstead now virtually reclaimed by the forest. Madeline barely recognized his skeletal visage as he stood before her.

John sold his land and took Madeline east to seek out the family of his widow. In Charlotte, he found the Clarke family and presented Madeline to them along with all the proceeds from the sale of his land.

Madeline stood silently and stoically as her father said goodbye and marched off into the wilderness once more. She did not give voice to the fear that she would never see him again.

John Carmack was last reported seen in an Indian village in the southern Ohio lands before disappearing into the untamed wilderness.

CHARLES TOWN, SOUTH CAROLINA 1675

DINISH MACCORMAC, SON OF WILLEM, A DESCENDANT OF RODNAN

inish sat in silence as the Privateer's ship sailed up the Cape Fear River and dropped anchor just offshore of a new settlement made up mostly of tents. He was now a free man, but with little in the way of possessions, he found himself to still be at the mercy of his masters.

Still, he looked on in wide-eyed wonder at the colonial seaport that would be founded for the English King and called Charles Town in four years. The English settlers controlled much of the land, and the planters brought in slaves from Barbados to start plantations and fuel the building of a seaport.

Dinish kept at his labors in Charles Town for nearly a year before once more meeting up with William Woodward, who had spent more than a year as a prisoner of Indians near St. Augustine. During his year of captivity, he had learned to speak their language and gain their trust by helping them to accomplish a thriving trade in furs.

In 1676 Dinish joined Woodward, agreeing to go on a series

of expeditions into South Carolina's interior developing relations with the various Indian tribes. They mainly dealt with the Westo Indians and the Shawnee, who were known as the Savannah Indians. Dinish would spend most of the next fourteen years working with Woodward until Woodwards' death in Charles Town in 1690.

CHARLES TOWN 1690
DINISH MACCORMAC, SON OF WILLEM,
A DESCENDANT OF RODNAN

inish now found passage on a ship heading upriver to Dorchester, then west to Fort Moore along the Savannah River, and then moving on to Fort Augusta. From there, it was again upriver into the North Carolina wilderness and on into Virginia.

He made his way to Fort Charles in what would later come to be known as Richmond, where he met with the colonial militia commander. Upon their introductions, the commanders' expression changed so that Dinish fell silent.

The commander asked, "You said, MacCormac sir?"

Dinish smiled as he replied, "Yes, I have introductory papers from William Woodward with whom I am certain you are familiar. I worked with him for many years in the South Carolina regions."

The commander cleared his throat, "Are you familiar with a John Carmack? He's your spitting image?"

Dinish shouted, "My son is John MacCormac!"

Dinish was asked to sit down, and the grave tone of the commanders' voice sent a chill down Dinish's spine.

The commander well knew John Carmack's tale because he had led two search parties that spent weeks looking for the missing children.

Tears streamed down his face, and he held his head in his hands as he learned that his son had lived near Fort Henry, just twenty-three miles away from this very spot. That his son had been so near caused him tremendous grief, and he remained inconsolable.

For two days, he was torn between going to see his granddaughter Madeline or heading off into the wilderness searching for his son, who had now been gone for a year. He knew all too well the dangers of traveling in the wilderness areas after seeing any number of men killed by Indian attacks and himself having narrowly avoided such a fate on more than one occasion.

The commander tried to convince Dinish that going off in search of John was mere folly and that John had previously returned after a similar amount of time and that the prudent thing to do was to wait for his son's return.

With a heavy heart, Dinish decided to meet his blessed granddaughter and give John time to rejoin them.

"DON'T JUDGE EACH DAY BY
THE HARVEST YOU REAP BUT
BY THE SEEDS YOU PLANT."

ROBERT LOUIS STEVENSON

CHARLOTTE 1690
MADELINE CARMACK, DAUGHTER OF JOHN, GRANDDAUGHTER OF DINISH, A DESCENDANT OF RODNAN MACCORMAC

During the following three years, Madeline's' grandfather filled her head with grand visions of the beauty of the MacCormac ancestral home in Ireland as they awaited her father's return. Dinish's health declined rapidly following an early spring that sent a whooping cough epidemic throughout the city. Dinish would die peacefully in his sleep, sure in the belief that now he would finally reunite with his beloved son John.

Madeline suffered no lack of suitors, and at the age of sixteen, she succumbed to the charms of Bradley Wharton. Wharton was tall, handsome, and well mannered. He spoke softly of his business interests in faraway places such as New York, Boston, Quebec, London, and Paris. He also listened intently as she told him of her family history, replete with the tale of her father selling off his homestead and placing his young daughter into the care of her grandparents. She also told him of her beloved grandfather Dinish who had scrimped and saved nearly every penny he had ever earned as he tried to make his way back to his son only to find him gone into the wilderness.

Bradley Wharton was thirty-two on the day he married the sixteen-year-old Madeline. They headed towards Fort Charles as Bradley needed to further establish connections with fur traders to keep his thriving business interests supplied with goods.

Here they set up to live in an abandoned farmstead using Madeline's inheritance from her father and grandfather to get things going as Bradley's funds were currently tied up. He spent much of the next few years traveling as Madeline struggled to raise the four boys that resulted from his infrequent visits.

Bradley returned home one afternoon with empty pockets and whiskey on his breath. When Madeline calmly questioned him about his business, he flew into a rage, knocking her to the floor with a balled fist and following that with several kicks until he lost his balance, tumbled headfirst into the wall, and dropped to the floor unconscious.

Bradley seemed to have lost interest in continuing with his spurious tales of businesses or investments and preferred to spend his days in any establishment that would extend him enough credit to dull his mind. He fell in with a group of similarly disgruntled men whose business fortunes had also fallen on hard times, and together they drank themselves into various states where their failures could thus become bearable.

Madeline could feel the stares of neighbors and town folks as she walked past them. Mr. Peabody, who ran the general store, solemnly shook his head as he denied her any more credit due to her husband's already overwhelming debt. She held her head high as she headed home with nothing to feed her children.

Militia Commander Briggs showed up at her door with his hat in his hand, and his head bowed. "I regret to inform you that your husband is dead. Apparently, it was that homemade liquor that got to him." The commander cleared his throat and continued, "You will also need to come to the fort and attempt to clear up your husband's debts at your earliest convenience, ma'am."

Madeline looked him straight in the eye, "I have no funds with which to pay any debts. This land and our home are the only things left."

Madeline sold these remaining assets to settle her debts and retained a meager amount of the proceeds. She used these funds to move her boys far enough away so that they could start their lives anew. She dropped the Wharton name and returned to using her maiden name of Carmack and forbade her boys from uttering Wharton's name anymore to remove the stigma she perceived it to have upon them. Having had few interactions with their father over the years, the children soon lost any memory of him.

Her sons each grew tall and true and gave her grandchildren to dote upon. She spent every evening telling the little one's tales of an Ireland that she had never seen. She regaled them with the stories of their grandfather and great grandfather's travels across the sea.

"THERE IS NOTHING MORE ENTICING, DISENCHANTING, AND ENSLAVING THAN THE LIFE AT SEA."

JOSEPH CONRAD

GLASGOW, SCOTLAND 1695
CONALL MACCORMAC, SON OF CONNOR, A DESCENDANT OF RONAN

onall was one day into his sixteenth year as he set foot aboard the ship that was to take him to a new life in the American colonies. Early in the passage, high winds and heavy seas sent most passengers and some of the crew into spasms of sickness. Conall had spent much of his young life aboard skiffs and sailing boats on the River Clyde and felt quite at home on a ship at the mercy of Mother Nature's fury. The ship's Captain quickly pulled Conall aside and put him to work as one of his ship's crew, and he found himself aloft in the ship's rigging smiling from ear to ear as he held on for dear life among the raging winds and stinging rain. By the time the ship reached port in New York, Conall had found a love for life at sea and vowed to spend his life upon it even if it was the last thing he ever did.

Conall spent the next two years sailing up and down the Americas' coast on all manner of ships, including a three-masted Clipper, a two-masted Schooner, and a six-month tour aboard a Brigantine. He was relaxing in a darkened barroom near the port when he heard that Privateer Captain William Kidd was in port and seeking crew for his ship.

Captain Kidd had been sought out by William the Third, King of England, Scotland, France, and Ireland, and given a Letter of Marque and Reprisal which authorized him to capture ships, crews, and cargo from enemy nations. His ship the Adventure had lost its best crewmen shortly after sailing from England when they left to join two Royal Navy ships, and Captain Kidd was forced to seek out new sailors in New York. Conall guessed this to be a grand escapade and quickly signed on. Many of the newer crew members were less than desirable sorts and included smugglers and pirates interested only in the bounty and the treasures to be had.

They sailed heading to Madagascar, and after much conflict with his new crew and only a few small encounters with other ships, they made port in the Laccadive Islands off the west coast of India. Some of the crew began speaking openly of mutiny, and Conall stood at the Captain's side as Kidd put down the insurrection by killing the gunner and many others chose to jump ship.

Soon afterward, they attacked and captured a massive treasure ship which they took over and renamed the Adventure Prize. This ship had belonged to the British East India Company, and the powerful company forced the government to brand him as a pirate and Kidd found that no port would offer him refuge, and he sailed back to the east coast of the Americas.

Here during the night, while anchored off the coast near Cape Hatteras, Conall and two other trusted men slipped off the ship carrying two chests full of precious items with instructions to bury them at their earliest convenience. At first light, the Captain set sail for New York, hoping his powerful friends could offer him some protection and believing that the buried treasure could be used as leverage toward his release from the charges of piracy.

Captain Kidd was arrested and sent back to England for trial, where he was found guilty of piracy and sentenced to death by hanging for his actions. In May of 1701, his luck held no better as the rope broke on their first attempt at hanging him, and he had to wait while a second rope was fetched. After his death, his body was placed in a cage and left hanging off the Thames River as a warning to any who might conspire in future acts of piracy against England. Conall and his two mates lived quietly along the Carolina coast, keeping silent watch over their hidden plunder. After hearing of Kidd's death, they divided their treasure into three equal shares and went their separate ways.

Conall MacCormac settled into a calm life, sometimes fishing and occasionally searching wrecked ships off the Carolina coast. From these, he would "find" valuable items that could then be sold legitimately, thus allowing him to live a comfortable life without suspicion of illegal doings. He lived in this fashion for the next fifteen years but always longed to return to the sea and feel the dance of the ocean beneath his feet.

Conall then met up with one Edward Teach, now better known as Blackbeard, the pirate. Teach had once served as a privateer in Queen Anne's Navy during the War of Spanish Succession but had since turned to piracy and now commanded four vessels and counted nearly three hundred outlaws under his authority.

Conall was nearly the same age as the famous pirate and grew to like the man who stood six foot four inches tall and cultivated a long thick beard into which he would often tie burning matches or strips of hemp so the smoke would billow out around his face as they attacked some hapless ship. His ships flew a flag that featured a skeleton spearing a heart while toasting the devil. This was a way to use intimidation as a tactic, and ships often gave up without a fight at the flag's mere sight and the ruthless reputation of Blackbeard and his crew.

Conall was with Blackbeard after one successful voyage

of pillage and plunder. When they entered port in Jamaica, Blackbeard and his men headed straight to an inn where he was well known and at various times either celebrated or demonized. Here he met with a dark-haired beauty that fell into his arms amid howls of delight from his crew. Conall stood silently on deck by mid-morning as the crew arrayed itself before the Captain and his newest love as they took their marriage vows offered up by the first mate. Another crew member muttered under his breath that this was the ninth or tenth time he'd seen this ceremony performed, although always in a different port and always with a different woman.

Blackbeard took up living along the outer banks of North Carolina for a while but, the lure of the sea called him out again. This time the governor of Virginia had tired of his actions and sent a naval lieutenant out with two ships to hunt the pirate down. On November 22, 1718, the two naval ships were lured by Blackbeard into an inlet near Ocracoke Island, where they became grounded on a sandbar. Blackbeard and his crew quickly boarded the seemingly helpless ship where they were ambushed by the well-trained navy sailors hidden below decks. Several cutlass blows wounded Blackbeard before being shot by as many as five balls fired from muskets. His head was cut off and mounted on the bowsprit as a warning to other pirates and also because it was also needed as proof to collect the rather large bounty that had been placed upon it.

Conall had been aboard Blackbeard's ship, where he was wounded at the outset of the fighting and, due to his injury, had not been a part of the boarding party. As the word of Blackbeard's death circulated among the crew, several boats went over the side, and Conall was on one. He made it safely to shore and quickly made his escape from the authorities with his intimate knowledge of the area.

Conall moved from place to place for two years until he had made his way to Hispaniola, where he traded several treasures that brought him a nice sized plantation and a comfortable lifestyle. Here he settled down comfortably, found a local girl to hold in his arms, and contentedly lived out his days without ever going to sea again.

SCOTLAND 1697
ROBERT MACCORMAC, A DESCENDANT OF EDWARD, A DESCENDANT OF NIALL

obert's grandfather had sailed from Ireland to Scotland across the Irish Sea, up the Firth of Clyde, along Loch Fynn to Argyll and the coastal town of Lachlan where he fell in love and married a young girl and settled down. Now Robert was twenty-two, married with two children, and living in the house where he had been born. They lived with his aged and ailing mother, two of his sisters, and his two younger brothers.

All of them combined with working the plot of land that they depended upon for their very survival. The previous two years had been challenging, with barely enough food produced to allow them to avoid starvation. These crop failures had brought about a widespread famine where nearly one in ten people across Scotland died of starvation or malnutrition during this time. The people were desperately seeking some solution that could provide for a better future. Robert's mother and a younger sister both succumbed to this deadly combination.

It was amid this backdrop of anxiety and despondency that the Darien scheme came about. Money was raised throughout

Scotland, with both nobles and common folk giving what they could as an investment in their country's future. Approximately twenty percent of the wealth of the entire nation was put forward.

The plan was to establish a Scottish colony on the Isthmus of Panama to provide for easy trading between the Indies and Africa. This colony would be placed near a bay in an as-yet-undisclosed location sheltered from high seas and storms, where friendly Indians lived, and the land was fertile and ready for planting. Five ships were to sail loaded with colonists who would establish this settlement, and the appeal went out across the land for volunteers. Robert heeded the call to join in on this grand adventure along with his wife, Aileen. They would leave their two young sons with their other family, and they could be sent for once the colony was established and their future secure.

On the fourth of July in 1698, they were among the twelve hundred souls who boarded one of the fleet's five ships. Once on board, each of the passengers was given an envelope that revealed their future home's exact location. The voyage would take four months in total, during which time some seventy people perished.

Landing in Panama, they christened their new home Caledonia and quickly set about clearing land and building a fort. After some two months, they realized that they had chosen a poor spot with no access to a fresh water supply and the site had to be abandoned and another chosen in its stead. The process of clearing and building began anew. Food supplies were limited, and various tropical illnesses, including malaria and fevers, plagued them all. The native Indians were indifferent to the settlers and had little interest in trading food or needed supplies for the trinkets the Scots had brought with them for just this purpose.

In February, Aileen had grown so weak that she could barely stand. She would linger for ten days before passing in Robert's arms. By March, the colony's numbers had fallen by two hundred, and ten more people were dying each day from malnutrition and disease.

By July, all hope was lost, and the colony was abandoned, and all except six individuals who were too weak to move boarded one of the four remaining ships for the long trip home. One of the boats sailed to Jamaica where it was refused aid, two ships sailed for New York harbor, and the sole remaining vessel attempted the return to Scotland.

Prior to the return of the lone ship from the first expedition, a second fleet consisting of three ships and thirteen hundred additional settlers had already set sail. Discouraged upon their arrival to find the disarray of an abandoned settlement instead of a thriving colony caused their morale to plummet. Deaths occurred due to the same diseases and poor diet that besieged the first expedition. Huts were rebuilt, but progress was slow, and disagreements among the leadership caused more dissension. Spanish forces attacked their beleaguered fort and held it under siege for nearly a month before they were forced to surrender.

Robert was among only a few hundred who would survive the adventure and manage to return home. Those who did return were considered a disgrace to the entire country that was now financially devastated from the enormous losses incurred by the failed expeditions. Having invested virtually all of their monetary worth in the scheme, many communities vented their anger at them. Many, including Robert, were disowned by their very own families and forced to fend for themselves among the hostilities of their countrymen.

"WAR DOES NOT DETERMINE WHO
IS RIGHT, ONLY WHO IS LEFT."

BERTRAND RUSSELL

NEW YORK HARBOR
MID-JUNE 1775
PATRICK, RYAN, AND DANIEL
MACCORMAC, DESCENDANTS
OF AIDRIAN

T he three MacCormac brothers stood excitedly at the ship's railing upon which they had just completed a voyage from their home in Ireland. Patrick, at twenty-two, was the oldest, and he playfully rubbed Daniel's head as he shouted, "You can smell the opportunity now, can't you?" Daniel, the youngest at just eighteen, grinned and replied, "I thought that smell was just Ryan." Ryan punched him in the arm, jumped back a step, and raised his fists, "Now I'll box your ears me boy-o."

They watched the city grow larger by the moment with a mixture of awe and wonder tinged with the exhilaration and unbridled optimism of youth. Each of them had a cloth bag sitting· at their feet that contained their entire complement of worldly belongings, and they were bouncing on their feet in anticipation as the ship pulled up to the dock that bustled with a myriad of activities. The Atlantic journey also brought many families from grandparents to infants, all abandoning their homeland and only allowed to bring one small suitcase or cloth sack apiece. Of course, some came with only the clothes upon their backs.

They waited in line with as much patience as they could summon while the port officials examined each passenger and their documents thoroughly. The process took some time as a large crowd of onlookers watched the proceedings with an air of enthusiasm. Some passengers were met by relatives or sponsors of their respective journeys; others were met by a retinue of peddlers selling a wide variety of wares. Still, others anxiously eyed those like the three young brothers.

Two well-dressed gentlemen stood on either side of a small folding table behind which sat a beguiling young woman who fanned herself gently and smiled in a coquettish manner. Her dress was cut low in the bodice, allowing her ample bosom to come under the admiring stares of the majority of the men who passed by. Upon the table was a stack of papers and a rolled-up document of some sort.

The men standing each beckoned the trio of travelers over with smiles and warm hearty handshakes and an enthusiastic, "Welcome to America, the land of opportunity. This is the place where your dreams can come true if you're willing to work hard."

The boys could hardly contain their smiles, and Daniel replied, "We can work hard."

"I'm sure you can lads, I'm sure you can," the man leaned in conspiratorially and lowered his voice slightly; "Tell me, boys, what prospects do you have lined up?"

The brothers looked at each other with questioning expressions upon their faces as the man continued, "Do you have family back home?" He didn't pause for their answer but kept on speaking, "Do you hope to have them join you here one fine day? Do you want to own your own piece of land boys? Your own piece of land, debt-free and beholden to none!" Without a word between them, the boys all nodded together in agreement.

"I can help you in achieving this dream, my friends," again he lowered his voice as he added, "You know we've been having a spot of trouble with those damned Brits …. Say you're not loyal to the redcoats, are you, boys?"

They quickly and without hesitation, affirmed that they were not.

The man beamed a grand smile at them, "Of course you're not, of course, you're not. Now take a look at this, my friends, take a look at this."

He moved over next to the lady who now sat with her hands folded primly in her lap. He then leaned down over the table and slowly unrolled a map of America as he spoke once more to his rapt audience, "This is America boys, wide open and untamed and waiting for YOU! Wide-open swaths of land that could be yours, yours, boys. Would you like that? Of course, you would, why who wouldn't. Now prime land like this, well, it's not just given away free. You've got to earn it, work hard for it, and I know you boys can do that. I can help you boys; you see, the Colonials are raising an army, a militia to fight against the English. All you have to do is sign up boys, and when the fighting is done, and that could be any day now, when it's over, you'll receive a bounty of land. Land of your choosing, free and clear for you and your family forevermore. Now, what do you think about that, boys?"

The girl now clutched three pieces of paper to her chest as she leaned forward.

Daniel replied, "Where do I sign up?"

Patrick put his hand on Daniel's arm, "Hold on now Daniel."

Ryan spoke up, "I'll not be joining up for no army. I didn't come over from Ireland to go and get into somebody else's fight."

The man calmly took one of the papers from the woman and held it up, "Land boys, the land you've always dreamed of, just waiting for you, but you have to earn it fair and square. Hell, you'll probably never even see a redcoat."

Patrick asked, "How long do we have to stay in this here army?"

The man replied, "One-year enlistment but, it most likely won't last that long now that they named George Washington as Commander in Chief of the Army. Don't forget that you'll also get six dollars a month pay."

Daniel stood staring at the smiling girl and again added, "Where do I sign up?"

Patrick looked over at Ryan and shrugged his shoulders, "Can't let him go by himself, can we?"

Ryan emphatically stated, "Not me, no sir, no way."

Daniel was now looking over the enlistment papers as Patrick tried to convince Ryan that it was the right thing to do. In the end, Patrick would join his youngest brother and enlist in the continental army while Ryan was bound and determined to find his own way in this new land of opportunity that was America. Ryan had heard too many tales of the frontier and the men who were even now living a life filled with adventure and building a future for themselves and their families, and he did not want to miss out on a chance to join them.

"THE SOLDIER ABOVE ALL OTHERS PRAYS
FOR PEACE, FOR IT IS THE SOLDIER
WHO MUST SUFFER AND BEAR THE
DEEPEST WOUNDS AND SCARS OF WAR."

DOUGLAS MACARTHUR

DELAWARE RIVER NEAR TRENTON NEW JERSEY
DECEMBER 1776
PATRICK AND DANIEL MACCORMAC, DESCENDANTS OF AIDRIAN

The brothers MacCormac huddled around a small campfire with six other soldiers and stamped their feet in a vain attempt at warming them. Patrick had toes poking from the ends of each of his shoes, and Daniel had lost the entire sole from his right shoe, and still, they were better off than four of the other men in their little group who had no shoes at all. Two of the men shivered in the bitter cold from which they had no shirts to protect them. None of the eight soldiers had a blanket or a coat, and none had the protection of a tent or hut to shelter them from the elements. All of them were gaunt from the poor diet, and most of them suffered the effects of typhus or some variation of pneumonia.

A sergeant came by and issued them their food ration for the day, and it consisted of one ball each of a doughy mixture that was then thrown directly into the fire to cook. The so-called "fire cakes" would be flipped over at some point and generally came out of the fire burnt and ashy on the outside and often uncooked in the center.

Gone was the boyish optimism and patriotic zeal that had marked their early days in the army. They had felt quite at home as nearly half of the men in this new army were Irish, and a good many of the officers were also natives of their former homeland. While they were marching and drilling and learning the rudiments of soldiering, the British had driven the Americans from Breed's Hill during the battle of Bunker Hill. It would be a long hot summer and then a brutally cold winter and marches through deep snow followed by fights where each of the brothers first fired a shot at an enemy who was also trying to do them mortal harm. Patrick was upset because he was sure that his shot had missed, and Daniel was upset because he was certain that his shot had hit its mark.

As their second summer in America turned into the cooler days of autumn, the boys found themselves involved in the Battle of Long Island. The two armies skirmished throughout the day, and the colonials fell back until they were surrounded and nearly captured. They felt fortunate to have escaped with the majority of the army during the dark of night. The English captured the city of New York, and a few weeks later, the Americans were forced to retreat from White Plains, New York. The Hessian troops captured Fort Washington, New York, while British Lord Cornwallis also took Fort Lee as the winter weather assault began.

So the boys were now battle-hardened veterans as they chewed upon their fire cake dinner and waited for orders from General Washington. On Christmas Eve, they received a prized stack of gifts in some thin, tattered blankets and woolen socks so that each man among their unit was in high spirits when word came on Christmas morning that they would attempt a night crossing of the ice-choked Delaware River. After which, they would attack the main body of fourteen hundred Hessian troops encamped in Trenton. Patrick had given his new pair of socks to Daniel as his feet were nearly frozen, causing him significant discomfort.

As darkness fell and Christmas day came to a close, General Washington and his twenty-four hundred men boarded cargo vessels and flat bottomed ferries for the three hundred yard crossing of the river in a blinding snowstorm. Like most of the men, Patrick and Daniel chose to remain standing during the crossing in an attempt to keep their feet and their new socks dry. Upon reaching the shore, the troops formed up for the nearly ten-mile march into Trenton. After about five miles, Patrick had to carry Daniel as his feet had become frostbitten, and it had become too painful for him to walk.

Patrick continued carrying Daniel while consoling him as best he could, "Hang on, Danny Boy, hang on me boy-o." Daniels' only reply came in the form of cries of pain and anguish. It was only when Daniel fell silent that Patrick stopped and laid him down gently in the snow.

"Come on now Danny Boy…," he leaned in close as he rubbed his hands over his brothers' chest, arms and shoulders, "We'll be home soon, strolling through the green fields with a girl on each arm and a pint waiting for us in the pub. Now hold on my brother, hold …," He fell silent as he lightly brushed his fingers over Daniel's face. He leaned in close and kissed his brother on the cheek before falling back in line with the other men trudging along.

The German mercenary soldiers never believed the Americans would dare attempt an attack in this inclement weather and were soundly defeated with many of their supplies and soldiers captured and transported back across the river.

Daniel's body was left in the snow beside the road along with numerous other soldiers whose losses were not caused by the enemies' actions. Indeed, it was true for the entire war that several men would die of disease or other causes for every one killed by their opponent. That was of little solace to Patrick as he contemplated life without his baby brother and lifelong companion.

Patrick had his one-year enlistment extended to three years as the war continued. Battles were won, and others were lost, and through it all, Patrick became numb to the scenes of death and destruction that occurred all around him. As the seasons rolled by, he received his orders and followed them without question and had long since lost any sense of compassion for the men he aimed his weapon at or the dead or dying men he stepped over on the battlefields.

Patrick continued as the humanity drained from his soul and seeped out upon the bloody grounds that had become the theatre of war. He stood dispassionately as he was offered a chance to reenlist at the completion of his three-year tour of duty. Instead, he just dropped what little gear he had, stuffed his discharge papers in his pocket, and marched out of camp as a civilian.

He walked for nearly a week before the cloud that covered his mind began to part enough to allow in a glimmer of sunlight. At last, he thought of Ryan and recalled that he had told them of his being in Kentucky and a friend of the legendary Daniel Boone in a letter from more than a year ago. Patrick smiled for the first time in ages and set out for the frontier.

BOONESBOROUGH, KENTUCKY 1775
RYAN MACCORMAC, A DESCENDANT OF AIDRIAN

It hadn't taken Ryan long to head south from New York, setting his sights on the Carolinas. It was here that he first heard the stories about a frontiersman named Daniel Boone, whose son had been tortured and killed by Indians just two years ago.

He had been commissioned into the Virginia Militia a year ago as Lieutenant and then a Captain and been placed in charge of three forts. Boone was chosen by George Washington and appointed to guide thirty surveyors out of the Kentucky Indian territory and back to Virginia's safety.

Although King George had expressly forbidden westward settlement over the Appalachians by the colonists, Boone led settlers into the Kentucky wilderness through a notch in the Appalachian Mountains called the Cumberland Gap. The four hundred mile-long trail would become known as the Wilderness Trail, and more than three hundred thousand settlers, including Ryan, would follow in the years to come.

In 1775 they built a fort and settlement that became known as Boonesborough, and settlers flooded in to claim land. They came from Ireland, Scotland, England, and all parts of Europe as the Shawnee nation watched the white men come in and take over their lands. Ryan learned how to live and survive in the wilds and was greatly surprised when he found he was a crack shot with a Kentucky Long Rifle like the one carried by Boone. Boone named his rifle Tick Licker because he said he could shoot a tick off an animal without hurting the animal.

Ryan sat and listened to the tales that Boone had killed a panther at age twelve and a bear with only a knife at twenty-six. They also said that even though the Indians had killed his son, he was sympathetic towards their plight and thought they were unfairly treated. Ryan could not wait to get to the fort at Boonesborough and arrived there in the winter, where he quickly fell in as a productive member of the settlement. He proved himself by providing game to eat and even took a few turns trapping beaver.

In the spring, Boone's daughter Jemima and two other girls were captured by the Shawnee and taken prisoner. This was a great fear among the settlers, and Daniel grabbed Ryan and a few others, and they rushed off after the girls and their captors. After tracking them for days, they attacked the tribesmen and liberated the girls to much acclaim. Word of Boone's daring rescue attempt further added to his growing legend. It would eventually lead writer James Fennimore Cooper to immortalize it in the fictional account "The Last of The Mohicans" with Boone as the inspiration for the main character.

Ryan could not escape from the war that raged in the American lands, and as his brothers fought in the east, he would face the Indians who were being armed by the British and encouraged to fight against the settlers. The war chief of the Shawnee was a fierce warrior named Blackfish, and he accepted the arms that the British offered and then set about to attack Boonesborough.

Boone led a force of thirty men out from the fort to seek the salt they depended upon for their very survival. They had been camped for some time and working hard to prepare the salt when Blackfish and his warriors captured them. Boone and his men were taken to the Shawnee camp, and as the white men huddled together surrounded by menacing tribesmen, other warriors formed two long lines where they swung war clubs and small hatchets amid blood-curdling war cries. One man was pushed out and forced to run the gauntlet. He was quickly knocked to the ground and beaten without mercy until he lost consciousness. A rider on horseback then took him by the foot and dragged him some distance away.

The remaining men fell back amongst themselves after witnessing that event, and it was then that Boone stepped forward. He took a long look at Blackfish and then charged into the gauntlet and knocked one warrior to the ground while wrenching the tomahawk from his grasp. Jumping to his feet, he moved down the line, fighting first one and then another of the warriors until, at last, his captors hailed his bravery, and the fighting turned into a celebration of his spirit. The Shawnee and Blackfish adopted him and came to think of him as a brother.

Ryan and several men escaped and headed off into the wilderness, finally making it back to the fort. Still, Daniel and the other men remained as prisoners for four months until Boone could escape. He made it the one hundred and sixty miles to the fort at Boonesborough in four days and warned them of an imminent attack.

As Boone and the settlers were preparing for the Shawnee attack, a new group of some fifty pioneers arrived. Among them was a war-weary twenty-five-year-old man whose eyes searched each man he passed in the hopes that one of them would be the familiar sight of his brother. As Patrick forlornly looked for a remembrance from the past, he leaped to his feet at a vision from the present. Ryan strode through the front gate of the fort dressed in buckskin clothes from head to toe, a rifle across one shoulder, and a string full of rabbit and assorted small critters hanging over the other. Ryan let out a holler and raced over to his brother and jumped into his arms.

Ryan shared his stories with his brother, and they drank a toast to Daniel. Patrick tried several times to talk about what he had seen and done but fell silent each time before he could find the words.

The Shawnee outnumbered the settlers by seven to one and soon began an eleven-day siege of the fort. Patrick picked up his rifle and joined in the fort's defense, but his demeanor soured, and not even the presence of Ryan could push the demons from his head. Still, the Shawnee were unable to defeat the settlers or force them to leave the fort, gave up the attack, and retired back into the forest.

Plans to pursue the Shawnee were formed but, Boone refused to participate as he felt it was an act of revenge and did not want to be a party to it. Patrick handed his rifle over to Ryan and told him he would never use it against a man again, for his heart could not take it. Ryan took part in the campaign against the Indians and was there when Blackfish was killed.

Ryan would marry a Scots-Irish girl who had made the journey from Ireland with her parents, and together they would build a home among the wilderness and raise five girls and five boys.

Patrick stayed in Boonesborough and lived quietly, keeping mostly to himself. He would never marry nor have children, although Ryan would bring his children over on occasion so they could visit with their solemn uncle. Some years later, Patrick stopped talking entirely and was often seen walking about holding silent and animated conversations with companions that no one else could see. Patrick was not yet forty, although many took him for a man of nearly sixty. Ryan ended up taking him into his own home, where his brother continued with this strange behavior until one night, at the age of thirty-eight, he passed away in his sleep and was finally free from the demons of his past.

"A SMALL BODY OF DETERMINED
SPIRITS FIRED BY AN UNQUENCHABLE
FAITH IN THEIR MISSION CAN
ALTER THE COURSE OF HISTORY."

MAHATMA GANDHI

PORTSMOUTH, ENGLAND
MARCH 1787
PATRICK MACCORMAC,
A DESCENDANT OF AIDAN

atrick MacCormac beamed as the midwife handed him the tiny bundle wrapped in a green blanket. A shock of red hair graced the head of the newly born Sean. He leaned down and kissed his wife Erin and placed the baby back in her arms. He decided it was time to celebrate the birth of his firstborn son. They had come to Portsmouth two years earlier so that he could ply his trade as a shipbuilder, and indeed he had quickly found employment.

Patrick staggered out of the pub to find the daylight rapidly fading away and decided it was time to head home. He hadn't gone far when he stopped in the middle of the lane, unbuttoned his trousers, and proceeded to relieve his swollen bladder on the spot.

As he turned to continue about his way, he found himself staring into the eyes of a grinning constable who spun a small wooden nightstick that hung from a leather strap attached to his wrist. "What have we here?"

Patrick opened his mouth to speak, but the words seemed to jumble up in his mind, and he just stood silently swaying slightly to and fro. For reasons that he later could not fathom, he bolted away from the constable who stood firmly in place, watching him stumble away.

Patrick made it about twenty paces before he slipped and fell. Lying on the ground, he looked up at the constable's still smiling face and attempted to tip his cap, but his cap was nowhere to be found. He regained his feet with some effort, and after calmly brushing the dirt from his sleeves, he took off at a run.

The constable swung his arm and let the nightstick fly from his grasp. It hit Patrick in the middle of the back, and he tumbled headfirst through a storefront window.

When Patrick awoke the next morning in jail, he had little memory of the previous evening's events. Two days later, he stood sheepishly before the aged magistrate who had no interest in hearing the pleas of yet another drunken Irishman, and in less than five minutes, he had determined his fate.

Deportation was ordered, and as the stunned Patrick was dragged from the room, Erin sat sobbing as she clutched their newborn son to her chest. Patrick was taken with five others to the docks where they were paraded past jeering crowds. They were led onto the ship Alexander that had just docked a few days prior on March 16.

Of whose number seemed to grow almost daily, Patrick and the other prisoners were shackled but otherwise treated well and given better food than some were used to. Patrick found out that the boat was destined for Australia.

Captain James Cook had, in 1770, discovered new land and named it New South Wales. He thought it would be a good place to colonize and reported this back to the government. By 1788 with overcrowded jails in England, it was decided to establish a penal colony in this uncivilized land.

Eleven ships in all would make up what would later be called the First Fleet. The ships would carry more than seven hundred and fifty convicts, including almost two hundred women along with some five hundred and fifty officers, marines, ship crews, and their families. They would be the first of nearly one hundred and sixty thousand convicts to be sent to Australia over the next seventy years.

The fleet would not depart on their fifteen thousand-mile journey until the middle of May; Patrick had now been on board for two months. They made stops in Tenerife, Rio de Janeiro, and Cape Town before arriving in Botany Bay eight months after departing from Portsmouth. After just a few days, it was decided that the site was unsuitable for settlement, and they moved along the East Coast, arriving at Port Jackson on January 26th.

Over the next two years, the settlers endured many hardships but eventually cultivated a few meager crops and began building new lives. Patrick was among many who were released from their sentences due to their good conduct.

Patrick was even allowed to send for Erin and Sean. They arrived some eight months later. Their family quickly grew larger as they helped in giving birth to a nation.

"NEVER THROUGHOUT HISTORY HAS A
MAN WHO LIVED A LIFE OF EASE LEFT
A NAME WORTH REMEMBERING."

THEODORE ROOSEVELT

AFRICAN SUB-CONTINENT 1805
AEDAN MACCORMAC, A DESCENDANT OF AIDRIAN

edan MacCormac had been born in Scotland of Irish parents, and since the age of fourteen, he had been at sea as a sailor who had been to many foreign lands aboard a variety of ships and was no stranger to exotic ports. Already an old sea salt at twenty-five, he now sat in a dark, dank sailors bar near the Portsmouth, England harbor. Always on the lookout for the next job, he picked up on a conversation about an expedition heading to Africa, and a smile came quickly to his face.

Mungo Park was a famed Scotsman who was a doctor and surgeon who had gone to Africa in 1795 on a two-year solo exploration of the Gambia and Niger rivers in deepest, darkest Africa. He had been believed to be dead and caused a genuine sensation when he emerged from the Dark Continent. He went on to write a bestselling book detailing his exploits and became a national hero. Now he had been invited by the government to lead another expedition.

Aedan joined Park's team along with nearly forty others and

boarded the transport ship Crescent in Portsmouth, heading to the Cape Verde Islands off the northwest coast of Africa.

On April 6, 1805, they arrived on the Gambia River, where it would take nearly a month to gather the needed provisions and supplies, including a few horses and many donkeys. It was the onset of the rainy season, and Park feared that any further delay would mean having to wait here for another six or seven months, so with that, they set off into the interior.

Almost immediately, the African heat caused the pack animals to bray under their heavy loads, and they refused to accommodate their masters. Progress was impossibly tedious and slow. It took days to acquire more donkeys to even out loads of cargo amongst the beasts. They were only a few days out when dysentery hit the camp, and several men fell ill.

The unusual sight of a large caravan of white men caused natives to come out in large numbers to view them. The men were ordered to be at arms at all times and even slept with loaded muskets.

Isaaco was a Mandingo priest who had been brought on to guide the expedition, and while trying to negotiate safe passage, he was captured by a native tribe and then flogged. Adding insult to injury, his horse was also stolen. Park took Aedan and a few others on a rescue mission. It took two days and threats of armed retaliation before Isaaco was returned, and the caravan quickly moved on.

A few days later, one of the men threw a rock at a strange creature in a tree and instead struck a beehive at an encampment. The disturbed bees swarmed through the camp, causing the men and pack animals to flee in all directions. In the commotion, the campfires spread to the surrounding bush and added to the confusion. It would take hours to get the camp back under control. They lost several pack animals, and nearly every man suffered from multiple stings. Aedan had been stung almost two dozen times, and his face and hands swelled up so that he had to be tied to Parks' horse as he was unable to walk.

By early June, the rainy season had arrived with a fury, and the hard rain pummeled them without mercy and made movement difficult for the men and torturous for the heavily laden animals. A dozen men fell ill with fevers such that they could not walk.

The expedition moved through the beautiful but rugged country and by July had reached the Furkumo River, having lost eleven men thus far. During July, they progressed slowly and at a significant cost to the men and beasts. Men dropped beside the trails, unable or unwilling to go on, and were left to be taken by the beasts or the natives or claimed by the jungle itself.

By July's end, Park had lost twenty men dead or murdered, and all of the original donkeys had died or been stolen and had to be replaced. Every remaining man had illness or injury, preventing him from being at full strength.

The constant downpours inevitably caused the rivers, streams, and lakes to overflow, and the caravan struggled to slosh and trudge through the fast-moving currents that surged across the very trails and paths upon which they ventured.

At the end of August, the expedition finally reached the Niger River. Park now had only seven men left, including Aedan. After three days of rest, they loaded into canoes and headed out onto the river.

They passed through rapids and past vast herds of elephant, rhino, and hippos that would occasionally charge at them. They were thankful that they hardly had to paddle in the swift currents that propelled them along at six or seven miles every hour.

Park sent offerings to Mansong, the King of Bambarra, who ruled over much of the country. Without his blessing, they would not be allowed to continue down the river toward the Congo and the Atlantic Ocean and eventually home. The king gave his approval for the expedition and promised them protection on their journey.

By mid-November, Park was left with just Aedan and two of

his original men. They also had one guide and three slaves. They stayed in the middle of the river, fearing attacks by the large herds of aggressive hippos along the banks and the warlike faces of the tribes peering out from the dense forests.

They were approached by three canoes filled with natives armed with bows and arrows and pikes. Park and his men scared them away with multiple musket shots. Two more attacks came with many natives killed by musket fire and Park losing his guide and one of the slaves.

The river narrowed in places slicing between rocks and stony islands that were often lined with tribesmen chanting and shaking spears in their direction. They had gone more than two thousand miles across Africa, and one thousand miles of that down the river when Park ordered them to stop and seek enough provisions that he hoped would allow them to complete the final leg of their journey without having to stop again.

Two days later, they paused on the river as it divided into three narrow channels. Park surveyed them and made his choice. The rushing river pulled them through rapids as natives threw spears at them and killed the two remaining slaves. The men would paddle for their lives; grab a musket and fire, then resume paddling, alternating between the two grave dangers.

The canoe lodged between two rocks, and the men struggled to free it from the river's mighty grasp. The natives grew closer and hurled their spears at the four remaining men, who now began throwing everything out of the canoe and into the river.

Still, the canoe remained firmly lodged. Park took hold of Aedans' arm, and all four men jumped into the river as a last desperate attempt at escape and find salvation. The natives raced along the rocks, but the mighty untamed river swallowed up the men without leaving a trace.

"WOE UNTO THE DEFEATED, WHOM
HISTORY TREADS INTO THE DUST."

———

ARTHUR KOESTLER, DARKNESS AT NOON

KABUL, AFGHANISTAN 1842
EDWARD CORMICK, A DESCENDANT
OF ALAIN, A DESCENDANT OF
AIDRIAN MACCORMAC

Edward Cormick sat before the fire, trying to shake the bitter Afghan cold from his weary body. He thought about home back in England, where he had grown up in the quiet town of Southend-On-Sea just east of London.

His ancestors had come from Ireland some four hundred years earlier, or so the story was told. They had lived in Ireland and been left in the care of an older sister named Winifred after their mother's death. Winifred had later left to heed the King's call to assist in the war with France, and she was never seen or heard from again.

After that, the family split up, with the children being sent off wherever they could find someone to take them in. At that time, a boy named Arlen came to find himself in London, and nearly four centuries later, Edward had been born. After an uncelebrated childhood, he had joined the military, where he looked forward to a life of clean uniforms, substantial meals, and warm beds, and perhaps best of all, regular pay.

He had been a part of the Army of Indus stationed in India for the better part of a year and had seen little action as yet. The British were concerned about Russian influence in Afghanistan and decided to send troops there to thwart any Russian attempts to invade. So Edward and twenty thousand British and Indian troops left India along with forty thousand civilians. They crossed through treacherous mountain passes of the Hindu Kush before marching into Kabul some months later.

The British forces set about building a new base for themselves in an area that would prove challenging to defend. Simultaneously, they helped to overthrow the current leadership and set up one that would decidedly be friendlier toward Britain. After all of the political intrigues had died down, all but two brigades were withdrawn back to India. Edward was among those who would stay in Kabul.

The following year, the Brits found themselves very unpopular with the Afghans. British soldiers were often coming under attack whenever they were outside of their base camp and in small numbers. A British diplomat came under attack in his residence, and he and his staff were killed, then the leader of the British contingent was murdered by the hand of the man they had helped place in power. The remaining British leaders were able to negotiate a treaty that allowed them to leave the city and the country.

On January 6, 1842, Edward and the others in the British party began leaving their base, planning to march to Jalalabad some ninety miles away. Forty-five hundred troops consisted of seven hundred British and thirty-eight hundred Indians and more than twelve thousand civilians in their column. The civilians included families of British and Indian soldiers, servants, workers, and many Indian camp followers.

Almost immediately upon leaving their compound's relative security, the rear of the column where Edward was stationed quickly came under fire from all quarters as heavy snow fell and a bitter, unrelenting wind blew. They would only make six miles in two days, and upon entering a narrow four-mile-long pass, they came under withering fire from the high ground on all sides. Edward was continually facing the fire, and there were numerous small skirmishes when ten or twenty of the Afghans would attempt an assault, each of these was thrown back.

By the end of the third day, they had made it through the pass but at the cost of three thousand of their number, many of whom had frozen to death or taken their own lives rather than submit. Many wives and children gave themselves up under assurances of their safety and were promptly executed by the Afghan tribesmen. By January eleventh there remained only two hundred British troops alive, and they with Edward among them vowed to fight to the last man.

On the evening of the twelfth, Edward sat with the remaining troops numbering twenty officers and forty-five-foot soldiers. Among them, they had only twenty rifles and forty rounds of ammunition. Edward had a small knife with a curved blade in one hand and a rock in the other as the Afghans rushed their position.

Edward and his comrades charged forward into the fray while another group of mounted officers attempted a run through to a village not far away. Every man was cut down whether on foot or mounted.

At the garrison in Jalalabad, British soldiers watched a lone rider being chased by several Afghan tribesmen and dispatched riders to his rescue. Assistant Surgeon William Brydon was covered in blood from a sword wound to his head as the riders reached him. One asked him, "Where is the army?"

"I am the army," was his reply. Upon reaching the gates and safety, the pony he was riding lay down and died. Brydon was to be the sole survivor of the British army's fateful march from Kabul.

"ALMOST THE WHOLE OF HISTORY IS
BUT A SEQUENCE OF HORRORS."

NICOLAS CHAMFORT, MAXIMS
AND CONSIDERATIONS

DUBLIN, IRELAND
SEPTEMBER 1845
JAMES MACCORMAC, A
DESCENDANT OF RONAN

James and his wife Eileen were tenant farmers living on a small patch of land outside Dublin. They had never met their English landlord, who had no desire to set foot in a place he considered culturally and socially inferior. Like most English, he thought the Irish to be filthy, violent, and lazy people.

James worked hard, trying to support his family of nine that included his mother-in-law and his wife's younger sister. Their sole crop was made up of potatoes, although unlike most, they also had two dairy cows and a small brood of chickens to help sustain them. They sold a large portion of their crops each year to be shipped to England and lived on the remainder as the potato was the central portion of their diet.

As James went into the fields on a bright sunny day in September, he found the leaves on the potato plants had turned black and turned down toward the ground. James had to cover his mouth and nose due to the terrible smell coming from the plants. This blight covered the land, and nearly half of the entire island's potato crop was lost.

Some farmers were hit harder than others and found they could not pay their rent; this forced some off their land while others had to sell off what little they had to feed their families. James was able to sell off their chickens to get them through until the next crop could be harvested.

The coming year brought more of the same, and the people became desperate as the famine spread far and wide. Those who had borrowed money against their future harvests could not repay their debts and were forced off their lands. A large variety of ailments brought about by near starvation included dysentery, typhus, scurvy, and cholera.

James had now sold off his cattle and every possession he could in order to remain on their plot of land. Eileen's mothers' legs and feet swelled until she could not walk, and then her face began to bulge. She lingered in agony for a week before she died of what they called dropsy. Two of the children withered away and subsequently died from dysentery.

James could only watch in despair as another year came only to bring another massive failure of the potato crop. Eileen could no longer cry any tears and sobbed in near silence as they buried two more of her children in the ground that had forsaken them. They would soon become another of the more than half a million who were evicted as tenant farmers during the famine. Nearly one-quarter of the island's population of eight million would die, many in mass unmarked graves.

James, Eileen, and their three remaining boys dragged themselves away from the piece of land that the boys had never been more than a mile from and staggered into the city of Dublin, hoping to find passage on a ship heading away from this barren land. The port was lined with ships, each offering passage to the distant lands of America and Canada. James collapsed while they stood in line, waiting for food, and he was carried into an alleyway where scores of others in various states of distress already lay. A young girl came by with some weak potato soup, but James could not keep this in his stomach. Eileen refused to eat and lay down on the ground beside her husband and held his hand as he took his last breath, then she sighed deeply and joined him.

Their boys, Edward, Robert, and James, were aged ten, nine, and seven as their parents departed from them, and they huddled together unsure of what the future might bring for them as penniless orphans. Edward told his brothers to stay where they were, and he would try to get them some food. They lay silently staring up to the sky as he headed off in search of something to eat.

Edward came across two younger children sharing a loaf of bread, and he stared at them hungrily, trying to decide if he should take it from them and run. He didn't notice the man come up behind him until the man grabbed him by the back of the neck and said, "What have we here?" He stared back up at the man in silence as the man smiled and asked, "Hungry boy?" Edward nodded yes as the man broke into a laugh. "Come with me boy, and we'll get you something to eat."

The man released his grip from Edward's neck and gently laid his hand on the boy's shoulder as they walked along. Edward wanted to run away from the strange man, but the hope of relief from the hunger pains in his stomach kept him moving forward. The pungent smells of food wafting on the breeze brought the boy to a state of excitement as the man led him into a well-lit building with large glass windows. They sat at a table, and before Edward could speak, a plate of food was placed before him, and he began to gorge himself as the man grinned with satisfaction.

Between mouthfuls of food, the boy answered the man's questions, explaining that his parents were now dead and he was in charge of his two brothers and that they had no one else to look after them. The man sat with his hands folded in his lap and stated, "Well, we will see to it that your brothers get a fine meal too, you can trust me."

When he could eat no more, the lady handed him a small basket filled with more food to take with him, and he thanked her as he followed the man out of the door. The man said, "We have just one stop, and then we'll pick up your brothers."

Edward had a bounce in his step now that his belly was full for the first time in as long as he could remember, and he smiled as the man whistled a snappy tune as they walked along the wharf near the rows of ships. They entered into a darkened doorway filled with dank, musty smells. Inside it was nearly pitch black, and Edward strained to make out his surroundings until a match was struck and a lantern-lit.

A dark oily-skinned man handed over a small pouch to Edward's new friend, who shook it once and deposited it in his coat pocket and said, "Nice doing business with you gents." At that moment, two men that Edward had not seen in the gloomy darkness stepped forward and grabbed him by the arms, and dragged him from the room.

Robert and James lay sleeping in the alleyway when they, along with six or seven others, were carefully and quietly picked up and carried away. Robert woke to find himself at a long table with a bowl of soup and a thick slice of bread before him, and he attacked the food as did the other forlorn assortment of children around him. After nearly finishing the soup, he stood up and began frantically looking around for James as a kindly looking lady came forward and calmly patted his head. He tried to explain about James and Edward while she nodded and whispered that everything would be alright as she encouraged him to finish his meal. The children were led into a room with several mattresses scattered about the floor, and he quickly collapsed upon it and fell into a deep sleep.

Edward woke up in total darkness before realizing that a rough woolen sack covered his head and quickly pulled it off.

He lay among many boys and men of varying ages, and his stomach did a small flip as the floor seemed to sway beneath him. He shuffled his legs only to find them heavy with shackles and chains that bound him to the others. One of the older men chuckled softly and in a gravelly voice said, "Welcome to the navy boy!"

Robert was jolted awake as the small craft he was on thumped abruptly ashore amid shouts in a language he didn't understand that seemed to come from a variety of different voices. He filed out of the ship's hold along with three other young boys and three girls, all of them were shielding their eyes from the brightness of the sun. In turn, each was roughly handed over the side of the boat and placed on the back of a horse-drawn cart that waited at the water's edge. Once they were all settled on the cart, the horse was given a lash with a long-handled whip, and with a jolt, they watched as the waters receded from their sight. The oldest of the girls whispered to Robert, "I think we're in France."

James, still lying limp, was carried onto a ship that soon would set sail for America. He hadn't been awake for more than a few minutes at a time over the last two days and slipped in and out of consciousness without any realization of his surroundings. The ship was only two days at sea when his lifeless body was slipped over the side of the boat in the darkness of the night. He had not been listed on any ships manifest, and no record would ever be made of the passing of one more unknown, unnamed Irish boy.

SOUTH AFRICA 1866
EDWARD MACCORMAC, SON OF
JAMES, A DESCENDANT OF RONAN

The ten-year-old version of Edward had been terrified to find himself in such a state with his legs shackled in irons aboard a ship on the high seas bound for some strange faraway place. He cried when he realized that his brothers were not with him and wondered if he would ever see them again. When someone would ask a member of the ship's crew where they were headed, they would generally get derisive laughter and a "You'll see" in return.

Three days into their voyage, a crew member who was only slightly older than Edward told them they were headed for Cape Town in South Africa. Edward had no idea where that was or even what to expect when they arrived, having never heard anything about Africa other than some story about lions. Every fourth day a small group would be unshackled from the rest and taken on deck for some fresh air, and Edward had contemplated leaping overboard at the first opportunity he was afforded.

Now, as he knelt next to the railing, he saw that the crew took little heed of him or the others and his chance at escape was at hand. He stood on shaky legs and held onto the railing. He remained frozen in place as he scanned the seas in every direction without being able to see anything but waves that rose twenty feet above the ship and then fell into even deeper troughs and cascaded off into the vast unknown. Edward sank back to the deck in defeat, knowing that a jump over the side was only certain death, and he still held out some hope of being reunited with his brothers and so temporarily accepted his fate.

Among the human cargo on this vessel were thirty-three males and twelve females, most between the ages of six and sixteen, although there were a few older men scattered amongst them. Only one young boy died during the ocean journey as they were regularly given food and water from their captors. Far from being compassionate or caring, the ship's captain saw them merely as a commodity that was only of value if delivered alive.

The ship dropped anchor just half a day out of Cape Town and lowered a small skiff over the side where ten pieces of the human consignment could be ferried ashore at a time. The transfer was done here, far from any prying eyes in the busy port town.

Their chains were removed and replaced by rough ropes looped from their ankles to their wrists and around their necks. The rope was then pulled tightly so that each wearer was forced to bend at the waist, and the ropes chafed at the skin wherever it touched their tender human flesh.

After being lowered into the small boat and rowed into the shore, they were then loaded into large carts pulled by massive oxen. There were several white men whose skin had turned brown from exposure to the African sun, and they all rode horses. Edward stared at the very sight of the black-skinned men who tied them up and loaded them into the carts. These men were rail-thin and wore little in the way of clothing and no coverings upon their heads or feet as they handled all the labor for their masters who pranced about on their mounts barking orders in a strange language that was partly English.

They traveled in this fashion for three days in a northeasterly direction through a desolate, barren landscape where about twenty of the captives or nearly half of the cargo was sold to a similar looking outfit. Four days later, a now-familiar transaction occurred, and a dozen more of the frightened souls were transferred into bondage for new masters. Edward was now left with only eleven others, including three terrified girls of seven or eight.

A few days later, they stopped, and Edward was released from his bonds, his neck, wrists, and ankles now bloody and raw. With two of the other boys and one of the girls, Edward was removed and placed in a smaller wagon pulled by a single ox, and they watched in silence as the two groups headed away in opposite directions. The four scared youngsters huddled together in fear of what life with these new masters might be like. Edward eyed everyone with caution and apprehension while trying to make some sense of their predicament.

Listening to conversations, he determined that they had passed through the Orange Free State, and they were now in The Transvaal not far from Pretoria. The Boers had settled these areas, European farmers now known as Voortrekkers or pioneers a few years before as a way to be free from rule by the British. They were primarily a mixture of Dutch, French, and German peoples.

The children were placed in a simple mud hut while the master sat atop his horse and explained their surroundings. "Here, there's no need for ropes or chains. There is nowhere for you to escape to as the Kalahari Desert nearly surrounds you to our north and west, and if the heat doesn't kill you, there are plenty of wild beasts that would gladly make a meal out of you. The Zulu nation is to the east, and they will do things to you that will make you pray for death. So do what's asked of you, and you'll receive fair treatment. Your only value is as an investment, we paid good money for you, and you need to work off that debt."

They worked in the nearly dry fields helping with subsistence farming to provide just enough food for the occupants to live. They also made various attempts at raising cattle. The white men went out hunting every day, and within a few months, Edward was being taken along with them. He found it exciting to watch the hunts take place, and he took a spot as a beater, marching in a single file with the blacks through the bush, making noise intended to push the animals towards the hunters. Edward also learned how to skin and gut the beasts and remove the meat necessary for their survival.

One year passed into two, and although Edward was treated much better than the native blacks, he still was kept ragged and barefoot and living on the dirt floor in the rough hut. More years passed as Edward became a gun bearer for one of the master's sons whenever they went out on a hunt. On one such hunt, Edward mishandled the muzzleloader, and it accidentally discharged, killing one of the native boys who had been standing nearby. Edward dropped to the ground expecting the worst from his masters but instead, they laughed and patted his back in congratulations for his first kill in the bush. The group moved on, leaving the dead boy's body lying where it fell.

When Edward reached sixteen, he was allowed to move into the servant's quarters of the master's house and given a shirt and his first pair of shoes in more than six years. He was slowly introduced into various mining operations aimed at ores and valuable minerals and the years continued to slip past.

Edward was given his freedom and a small spot of land where by the age of twenty-two, he had a little wooden shack of his own and a half-breed woman who kept him warm on cold nights. The woman was legally considered "coloured" due to being half white and half native black African. After two years with Edward, she became heavy with child. She died giving birth, but Edward lovingly took his newborn son in his arms and gave him the name of Adam.

Time continued its march forward for nearly eight more years while Edward worked his way up from a mine laborer to a mechanic, to a position as a miner, and then a clerk before taking over as one of the mines officers. He struggled to save small sums of money in the hopes of one day heading back to Ireland and reuniting with his brothers even though he knew that there was very little realistic hope of ever finding them again after nearly twenty years. He lay awake at night wondering if he would even recognize them if he did find them and what would they think of the life he had made for himself in this foreign and often inhospitable place. He never shared any of these thoughts with his growing son and avoided answering any of the young Adam's questions about his past as if not speaking about them would ease any pain that he might have felt.

A young boy of fifteen was walking along the banks of the Orange River near Hopetown when he saw a small stone that appeared transparent. Erasmus Jacobs picked up the rock, looked it over, dropped it in his pocket, and then headed for home. His father was unsure what it was and showed it to a neighbor who did not know what it was. They dropped it into an ordinary envelope and mailed it off to a man who knew about gems and minerals. It was then that it became known as The Eureka Diamond, the first and perhaps most important diamond in the nation's history.

Hopeful miners carrying their picks, shovels, barrows, hammers, and drills hurried in from all over South Africa, and Edward was among them. He soon had a camp set up employing many natives in the alluvial mining operation, sorting and sifting and washing in the search for the elusive gems.

The Eureka discovery also set off a diamond rush that brought thousands of prospectors from around the world to South Africa. Funds poured in from England, France, and Germany as land prices soared overnight and labor shortages soon followed. Laborers poured in from India as the native blacks sought higher wages and better living conditions. The need for roads, railways, harbors, houses, and hotels became apparent, and a construction boom followed.

Those who did come found brutal heat in the summer, little water or fresh vegetables, and primitive and unsanitary conditions in which to live. There was also a rapid rise in tuberculosis, scurvy, and large numbers of accidents from rock-falls and cave-ins from the explosives used with little regard for worker safety. It was not an unusual sight to see workers drop dead and their bodies just tossed aside or stepped over in the charge to take his spot.

Edward used his years of mining experience to rapidly have his operations going full tilt while the rush was just getting started. His efforts began to pay off as he began accumulating a sizeable collection of smaller diamonds. Just as the frenzied dash for the diamonds was reaching full steam, Edward's crew pulled a large cache of medium-sized diamonds from the gravel and mud, and he fell to his knees and looked to the cloudless sky as tears tumbled down his cheeks.

Over the coming twelve months, they found less and less of the high-quality diamonds worthy of the cost of the mining operations. He pondered several high dollar offers from various speculators as each bidder tendered new propositions. Edward finally accepted an offer, cashed in virtually all of his diamonds, and finished making plans to return to the Ireland of his birth. Having left as a ten-year-old impoverished, orphaned child taken away and forced into illegal bondage, he planned a triumphant return as a wealthy man now hoping to find his brothers and return them all to the lands of their birth.

He booked first-class passage for himself and Adam from Cape Town to Dublin and stepped ashore as a confident and self-assured thirty-three-year-old man of means with his arm draped around his nine-year-old son's shoulder. He found little that resembled the few remaining visions he had of the past. He walked the streets and spoke to several people, but few could recall three small boys from so many years ago from among the million or so people who left the island to find their futures elsewhere. Some were all too quick to offer help to a man willing to pay to find his lost relatives, but none could provide results.

Edward rode from the city proper, unsure of the direction he should take. Whether from the trauma of his leaving or some other reason, he found that he could not recall even the name of the town of his birth, nor where in relation to Dublin that it might be. So he rode south to Glen Cullen, then west to Bathcoole and Newcastle, turned north to Clones, Ballycoolane and Garristown before heading east back towards the coast. In towns and villages all along the way, he looked for visual clues that might help lead him home but, nothing seemed to spur memories from his youth, and after four weeks of effort, he had lost all hope of finding his brothers.

All the well thought out plans of reconciliation and rejoicing were washed from his mind, and he sat sullenly and pondered his future. He had competing ideas of staking a new claim and starting life over here in this the land of his birth. Returning to South Africa and rejoining the fortune hunters now scouring the land or head to some other place such as America as she now tried to recover from the devastation caused by her Civil War. England, Scotland, and all of Europe also beckoned with the promises of new beginnings.

Edward finally ruled out staying in Ireland as he felt a deep pain in his heart from the painful memories it brought forth. He also decided that returning to South Africa voluntarily would somehow give validation to those who had stolen away his childhood and set him to live as a slave for so long. He considered sailing from Dublin to Le Havre on France's coast, where he could easily travel to Paris. Still, ultimately, the allure of a new beginning in the beacon of freedom that was America proved too hard to overcome. He booked them passage to New York.

PARIS, FRANCE 1847
ROBERT MACCORMAC, SON OF JAMES, A DESCENDANT OF RONAN

Robert was nine when he was taken against his will and placed aboard a ship that would carry him into a future not of his choosing. He cried almost constantly during the short journey from Dublin to the coast of France. Now he sat in the back of a cart with the six other children who had also been abducted and brought to this strange place.

The oldest of the three girls in the group was a ten-year-old named Mary, and she thought they were in France because she recognized the odd language that the people spoke. Robert could not understand a single word they said and feared that he was getting farther away from ever seeing his brothers again with each turn of the cart's wheels.

He was asked his name by a short, pudgy bald man holding several papers bunched up in his hands at one stop. Robert stated, "Robert MacCormac." The man got as far as writing Robert Mac when he stopped and indicated for him to repeat his name. After two more repetitions, the man still could not make out what the boy was saying. So wrote Robert MacIrish, which in his none to neat scrawl came to be read as Robert McIlroy that became his name according to his newly created "official" documents.

That night the cart stopped, and a tall, heavyset man with oily hair and bad teeth came to the rear of the cart. He stared at the children as he rubbed his chin. Finally, he made some muttered comments that brought howls of laughter from the other men standing nearby. He pointed into the cart and shouted out commands that caused two of the boys and one of the girls to be yanked roughly from the cart. Robert and the others remained huddled together in the farthest corner as the donkey pulling the cart resumed his plodding trek.

The children fell asleep despite their fear and the jostling that occurred along the rutted path they followed. Again, they halted just before dawn, and two men held lanterns up as they looked over the sleeping cargo. Quickly two more children were pulled from the cart, leaving Robert and Mary alone and wrapped in each other's arms.

As the first light of day broke free from the heavy clouds above them, they arrived at the edge of the River Seine and were loaded aboard a riverboat for the next portion of their journey. The children sat quietly, watching in wide-eyed wonder as the boat wound its way up the twists and turns of the river. The old man piloting the boat tossed them a small loaf of crusty bread that they hungrily devoured. The boat passed the bustling town of Rouen, which was as far up the river as the sea-going ships could travel before transferring their goods to smaller vessels such as the riverboat they were traveling in.

Mary whispered to Robert, "I think the old man said we're going to Paris, and I think that's the capital of France and lots and lots of people live there."

The boat came to shore near the small town of Sartrouville not far from Paris, and Robert and Mary were handed over to an older man and a large dull-witted boy of perhaps fifteen or so.

Few words were spoken as they walked along past rolling fields and wooded forests for almost an hour. They came to a small house set in a clearing not far from the banks of a meandering stream from which they could hear the sounds of what seemed like a large number of people at work.

Robert and Mary held each other's hand and did as they were directed while they held out hope that their new lives would be joyful and filled with happiness. They sat alone for some time before several people came over to join them; some gave quick smiles but most ignored their presence entirely. Finally, an elderly man with graying hair and a patchy beard walked up to the two newcomers using a stout stick for support as he did so. He began speaking very slowly in a deep growly tone. As he paused, Mary started to tell Robert what she thought he had said. As soon as she began to speak, the man swung his walking stick at her and bashed her across the knees while shouting violently. She curled into a ball as Robert wrapped his arms around her shoulders. The old man smiled malevolently and poked the boy in the ribs with the end of his cane once, twice, and then a third time until the boy had to release the girl from his grasp.

The man stepped between the two and forced them away from the protective comfort of each other's presence. He got close in so that the boy could smell the sour taste coming from his very breath, and he rattled on for several minutes. Even though he knew the boy did not understand the words, he was confident that the child would get the meaning. He then walked over and stood behind Mary while he stared at Robert. He reached down and cupped her chin in his hand and forced her head backward, and spoke directly to the boy in a threatening and menacing tone that clearly indicated that his failure to obey would result in her punishment.

Robert only got to see Mary for a few minutes a day and sometimes only in passing, and they rarely were allowed the chance to speak to each other. Robert was soon put to work doing all manner of odd jobs around the home and the small village where they lived and where no one dared to speak or even interact with him.

The old man who had once been a brick mason but had been out of work for a long time after an injury to his back had finally found work at his old profession, and he took Robert along as one of his assistants. Robert learned to mix the mortar and labored to carry the pails and the heavy bricks up the scaffolding. He was taught how to expertly put the brick in place so that the old man would not have to do any lifting. Any mistake or misstep on his part brought a swift reaction from the old man, often in the form of a backhand slap or kick that would knock him to the ground. The other workmen on the site turned a blind eye to the boys' maltreatment and kept their distance from the old man.

Robert continued at this for five years, and as he endured the punishment dealt out from the old man, his body grew firm from the constant labor. They were on yet another construction project as Robert was just one month shy of his fifteenth birthday when the old man spewed forth a string of angry epithets and swung the back of his hand at the boy.

This time Robert caught the old man's arm by the wrist and held it tightly as the old man tried to pull away. Robert leaned in close and stated emphatically that he would never take the abuse again. To make his point clear, he pulled the old man's wrist until he was forced down onto his knees. Robert released his wrist and roughly grabbed his chin, forcing his tormentor to look up at him. Robert spoke softly but forcefully, "I am no longer your property, and neither is Mary." His hand slid down the old man's neck, and he continued squeezing tighter and tighter as the resistance from the old man waned. Finally, he released his grip and left the man gasping on the ground.

Robert returned to gather Mary up, and they departed together that same day and headed into Paris with optimistic outlooks for their future. Soon they would each find suitable

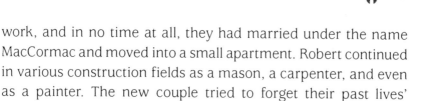

work, and in no time at all, they had married under the name MacCormac and moved into a small apartment. Robert continued in various construction fields as a mason, a carpenter, and even as a painter. The new couple tried to forget their past lives' travails and instead build upon what was yet to come. Mary filled Robert's heart with joy and their home with love as she gave birth to four little girls in the coming years.

Over the years, Robert had been involved in many projects and came into contact with many men in the construction business, and it was in this way that he met Frederic Auguste Bartholdi. Bartholdi was a sculptor looking for workmen to assist on various projects in which he was involved. Robert came to work for him at his shop in the center of Paris. He developed a friendship with the man who was also his employer.

In 1869 he traveled with Bartholdi to Egypt as the one hundred and twenty miles long Suez Canal was nearing completion. Bartholdi tried to convince Egypt's leader to allow him to design a lighthouse to commemorate the opening of the canal. This monument would stand at the canal's Mediterranean entrance and be in the structure of a woman holding a torch over her head while she would be dressed in peasant garb and entitled "Egypt Bringing Light to Asia." Plans were being drawn and designs worked on when the ruler went bankrupt, and the project was canceled.

Bartholdi went on to make some small changes, including making the woman into the Goddess of Liberty, and in 1875 he was commissioned to design the sculpture that would commemorate one hundred years of American independence. Bartholdi focused on the exterior design, and Alexandre Gustave Eiffel would concentrate on the iron and steel framework and interior skeleton of the structure. Robert first worked on many wooden structures before assisting with the multitude of plaster molds and casts needed. Finally, he also worked on forming the three hundred copper plates that weighed a combined eighty-eight tons.

Robert joined Bartholdi as he traveled to American in 1876 for the first official World's Fair. Known as the Centennial International Exposition, nearly one in five of the country's citizens or ten million Americans would become visitors. They would see the newest inventions such as Alexander Graham Bell's telephone, the typographic machine that would become famous as the typewriter. The sewing machine awed those home seamstresses of the day. They also could get the first taste of many new food items like popcorn, bananas, ketchup, and root beer. It was amongst this atmosphere that they set up the right arm and torch section of the sculpture so that visitors could see the magnitude of the planned work. They could also climb up a ladder to the balcony for just fifty cents, money that would become part of the fundraising needed for the project.

In Paris, the work continued as three hundred or more workmen labored on the undertaking. The statue was finally completed in July of 1884 and was put on display in Paris for nearly one year. It was disassembled, and the three hundred and fifty pieces were packed into two hundred and fourteen crates and shipped off to New York, where they arrived in June of 1885. Robert was one of the many workmen Bartholdi brought with him from France for the four-month effort to reassemble Lady Liberty and ready her for the late October dedication ceremony.

The ceremony was a grand success, and now the workmen could finally relax and enjoy their visit to New York for a few days before beginning their return voyage to France. Robert took the opportunity to get his hair cut short in the fashion of many in this bustling cosmopolitan city, and at the last moment, he decided to have his thick beard and mustache shaved off. Feeling quite at ease with his new look, he decided to take a long stroll among the thousands of the city's residents and visitors who lined the shoreline to stare out at the Statue of Liberty where she stood as a beautiful beacon in the harbor.

He stood, smiling at the sight that he had a small part in

helping to bring to reality when he felt the presence of a man off to his side. He turned to find a man staring at him intently. Robert tried to recall if he knew the man and guessed that he did and that it was he with his hair cut short and his facial hair removed that would have caused the consternation as to his identity. Still, the man looked at him with a puzzled expression, and then rubbing his eyes, he looked down and then away into the distance.

Robert smiled and approached the man and gently tapped him on the shoulder. When the man turned, and they were now just a foot or more apart, both men stared silently at each other. Finally, the man spoke softly as tears filled his eyes, "Is it possible... Robert, is that you?" Robert found it hard to breathe and asked questioningly, "Edward?"

The long lost brothers flung their arms around each other in a mighty embrace, pausing only to take a moment to stare into each other's eyes and then resume their hold upon each other. They sat, and each began sharing the details of their lives since that day nearly forty years ago when they were torn apart. Each wondered about their baby brother James, and their hope soared that he too might be found and that they could all be reunited.

They hardly spent a moment apart in the coming days as they tried to wash away the pains of the past and decide what they should do with this miraculous and now life-altering meeting.

"ALL THAT GLITTERS IS NOT GOLD."

ENGLISH PROVERB

SYDNEY COVE, AUSTRALIA
FEBRUARY 1851
JACK MACCORMAC, A DESCENDANT OF
PATRICK, A DESCENDANT OF AIDAN

As his neighbors knew him, Jack-Mac was a struggling farmer barely scratching out a living for his wife Rebecca and their young brood of five children when he heard the first rumors of a gold strike near Bathurst in New South Wales. A few months before that, he had heard tales of gold being found in Queensland and had even then contemplated going off in search of his fortune, but Becky had begged him not to go, and so he had stayed.

Even here in remote Australia, news had spread of the famed gold strikes in the American state of California. Just two years earlier in forty-nine and the stories told how easy it was for the thousands who had struck it rich while prospecting in America. This time the lure of striking it rich and providing a good life for his family proved to be more than he could take. After hearing of the latest strike and deliberating for a day, Jack loaded up a cart that wasn't much more than a wheelbarrow with what he assumed were the necessary items for digging gold and set off on foot on the two hundred kilometer trek.

He pushed himself hard for four days and reached the area of the strike and found that dozens of others were already there, and so without taking too much time for contemplation of a plan, he chose a spot of land and staked his claim.

Three days later, Jack stood and watched with disdain as hundreds more men poured into the area that was now being called Ophir, so named for the famed city of gold mentioned in the Bible. Just like Jack, people had walked away from their farms, their jobs, and their families. Jack stayed at his task from dawn to dusk, rarely speaking to anyone as the lust for gold and the fear of failure drove him on.

As the days wore on into weeks, many found the idea of this type of back-breaking work distasteful and unappealing and quickly gave up and left. Those who had hoped to collect the gold nuggets casually found just lying about on the ground as they had been told, soon grew discouraged and returned from wherever they had come. But many others like Jack, who back home had no real prospects other than scratching at the earth hoping just for survival, would stay, and on occasion, someone or other would make a strike and pull the precious metal forth into the light.

Jack himself had just a few tiny nuggets to show for his efforts, and even these he kept hidden away from any prying eyes. Like everyone else, he had heard tales of some lucky soul who made a strike and then had to battle numerous claim jumpers and bands of thieves who chose larceny over mining as a way to monetary gain. Then, of course, there were the bushrangers, outlaws, and former convicts who preyed upon travelers with brutality and little compassion. It was through this gauntlet that a successful miner must pass to claim his just reward and cash in the golden prize he had struggled to liberate from the ground.

By August, gold had been found to the south in Victoria near a place the Aborigines called Balla-arat, and within a month, ten thousand hopeful miners were digging there. At almost the same time, just to the north of Balla-arat was Bendigo, where a woman found gold in a creek bed, and within a few months, there were twenty thousand more gold prospectors there.

Before the time the first discoveries of gold had occurred, Australia's population had been seventy-seven thousand whites, consisting mainly of convicts. In the following year, three hundred and seventy thousand people came, and they would be followed by one hundred and seventy thousand the next year. They came from England and Ireland and all over Europe. So many came from China that they were soon required to pay a tax upon their arrival.

Jack finally hit pay dirt when he unearthed a vein of the precious metal containing a single nugget about four inches around and nearly twenty inches in length. It stretched from the crook of his elbow to the tips of his fingers. As he brushed the dirt off, he had to resist the urge to let out a celebratory scream.

By this time, an assayer's office was set up locally that was open day and night to accommodate the large amounts of gold being brought in. Shipments were regularly taken back to the coastal towns and loaded aboard ships that then sailed to England.

Jack would eventually sell off his claim and settle down on a lovely large property in Sydney Cove from where he would live out his days comfortably with Rebecca and their children.

"Half a league, half a League,
Half a league onward.
All in the valley of Death.
Rode the six hundred."

ALFRED LORD TENNYSON, THE
CHARGE OF THE LIGHT BRIGADE

1854 CRIMEAN PENINSULA
COLIN MACCORMAC, SON OF CYRIL, A DESCENDANT OF PATRICK, A DESCENDANT OF AIDAN

yril MacCormac was a smithy working an iron forge and shoeing horses on the outskirts of Sydney, Australia. At the same time, his young son Colin dreamed of adventure and searched for reasons that would allow him some respite from the heat and drudgery of working the iron.

At any moment, he could find an excuse for hopping atop a horse and galloping off. Soon he was known as one of the best riders around and even entered and won many races, although technically, he wasn't old enough.

By age eighteen, he joined the British army stationed in Australia, and due to his riding skill, he soon found himself in the mounted Calvary. Colin loved military life as it provided camaraderie with his mates and the opportunity to ride every day.

As war broke out in the Crimean Peninsula in 1853, Colin and his cohorts champed at the bit to join in the fighting. A few months later, they would get their wish. Colin was involved in some minor skirmishes before being attached to the 17th Lancers as a part of the Light Brigade.

They were called a Light Brigade due to their light, fast and unarmored horses. The men were armed with lances and sabers. The Heavy Brigades rode large, heavy chargers, and the men wore steel helmets and carried cavalry swords.

On the morning of October 25, 1854, Colin and the 17th Lancers sat atop their mounts in the center of the line along with the other units that made up the Light Brigade. They formed up at the end of a mile-long narrow valley with hills on both sides that were in the hands of the Russian and Cossack forces.

Colin watched as Captain Louis Edward Nolan rode down to speak with Lt. Gen George Bingham, 3rd Earl of Lucan. He saw Nolan wave his arm in a broad sweep forward. Lucan quickly turned to Major General James Baudenell, 6th Earl of Cardigan, and ordered an immediate attack.

Cardigan set off charging forward saber in hand, and his six hundred and seventy men followed. Colin could not say if a bugle charge had been sounded for the thundering of hooves and the shouts of the men.

The Russian forces were fully dug in with fifty artillery pieces facing forward and more than five thousand cavalry troops standing at the ready. Both hillsides also had artillery batteries trained on the valley below.

Shortly after the charge began, Captain Nolan raced out front, and a shell exploded beneath his horse, killing him. The sporadic firing came from the hills until they reached a point three hundred yards from the Russian lines before the main artillery barrage commenced. The air was thick with grape and round shot. Smoke, dirt, and dust kicked up from the bombardment, making it difficult to see, yet even as men and horses fell all around, those still mounted rode on.

Colin had been hit with several of the small pellets that made up the grapeshot. Yet, he still made it to the enemy artillery batteries along with many others before they were repelled and forced to retreat down through the valley.

Colin spurred his horse, let his riding instincts take over, and he thought of this as just another race that he would have to win. Artillery shells and rifle fire rained down around him as he rode, yet he only felt the power of his mount and the beating of her heart as she valiantly carried him to safety.

Colin was one of only one hundred and ninety-five men still astride their mounts when the battle ended. More than three hundred men were killed, wounded, or captured, and three hundred and thirty-five horses were killed in the charge of the Light Brigade.

"WE LEARN FROM EXPERIENCE
THAT MEN NEVER LEARN
ANYTHING FROM EXPERIENCE."

GEORGE BERNARD SHAW

THE PACIFIC OCEAN NEAR
THE HAWAIIAN ISLANDS 1855
ALFRED MACCORMAC, A
DESCENDANT OF AIDRIAN

Alfred MacCormac was an able seaman who enjoyed long voyages at sea because they allowed him to clear his head of the memories that always reminded him about losing his one true love. Elizabeth had been a vision of joyous beauty in his eyes, and his heart beat fast and true whenever he occasioned to be in her presence. All it took was a fleeting glimpse or a furtive glance in his direction from the fifteen-year-old Liza to get his youthful blood flowing hot.

They were bound together in matrimonial harmony, anxious to build a family of their own, and longed to move out of the home they shared with her grandparents, parents, and assorted siblings. Still, their love allowed them to steal off to find comfort and intimacy in the woods nearby, and it wasn't long before she began to glow from the sprouting of life within her.

Alfred dropped to his knees as her screams cut through him like a knife. She writhed about in the bed made of straw as her mother and grandmother tried to comfort her from the distress caused by her child's birth. Despite their efforts, the child was born without life, and now their very own little girl started slipping away while they tried to console her. Alfred held her hand and whispered words of love into her ear as tears rolled down his cheeks, and her life and love drifted away on the winds of despair.

Ten years passed, and Alfred had become just another lost soul wandering through life. He bounced from ship to ship, port to port, and girl to girl amid a haze of rum or wine or ale. Often quiet and sullen, he was quick to show a violent temper or raise a fist and, as a result, was often given a wide berth by his shipmates. Although a competent and capable seaman, he rarely was asked to return for a second tour of duty aboard any vessel.

He stood alone and stared blankly out at the vast emptiness of the Pacific Ocean as he sipped on his daily ration of rum. His current ship had come around the Cape and made her way up the coast to California, where they had loaded up with barrels of whale oil and bales of animal skins. Now they sailed west headed toward the exotic ports of call in Asia and China, of which Alfred had only vague alcohol ravaged memories. First, they eagerly faced a stopover in the islands of Hawaii, where throngs of friendly natives and beautiful curvaceous women supposedly awaited them.

As they neared the Hawaiian Islands, a fierce storm raged about them and battered the ship so that the mainmast was split, much of the rigging was damaged, and the rudder suffered some as yet undiagnosed adverse effects. One of the footropes had come down during the blow, and two of the sailors aloft had been lost at sea, and another man standing near the bowsprit had gone over the side. All hands listened attentively as the Captain committed their mortal souls to the depths with a few passages from the Bible. Alfred remained impassive while the Captain spoke and paid no heed nor took any solace from his words. His only thought was that they might receive an extra ration of rum in honor of their lost mates, and this finally brought a rueful smile to his lips.

The ship limped toward the islands. After dropping anchor in the relatively calm waters of a sheltered bay on the northwest side of the island, they were quickly surrounded by dozens of large outrigger canoes of a type most had never seen before. The people were resplendent in colorful wraps and bedecked with ringlets of fragrant flowers, and many of these garlands were thrown up to the sailors who lined the decks in wide-eyed wonder. Alfred was among those chosen to accompany the captain ashore to parlay with the natives, and he was glad for the opportunity it afforded him to get a closer look at the native girls after so much time at sea.

One-third of the crew was allowed ashore, and this attracted a great gathering of the native peoples who brought forth a festive attitude and a multitude of foods and intoxicating sweet fruit-based drinks. Drums sounded, and the women danced while keeping their hips moving to the drumbeat's rapid pace.

The captain sat with the local chieftain that someone said was a member of their Royal family while the crew gorged themselves on the exotic foods laid before them. Alfred smiled broadly and even allowed himself to be pulled up from the sand to join in with a group of dancers who moved gracefully and with joy around a large fire on the beach.

Alfred settled back into his seat on the pure white sand and drank deeply from a wooden jug offered by a young smiling girl. He blinked several times, trying without success to clear the haze that had come over his vision, and he laughed loudly as he staggered to his feet. Just then, a young island girl walked past, carrying a tray of fruits, and Alfred grabbed her around the waist. This caused the tray and its contents to fall to the ground and the girl to give a small scream of surprise as Alfred casually tossed her over his shoulder and turned to walk away.

Two of the native men raced over and stood in front of Alfred as the girl squirmed to get free from his grasp. Alfred laughed, "Out of the way, me Buccos, this one's mine!"

The two men did not move, and the smile slipped from Alfred's face only to be replaced by an uncontrollable rage that erupted as in one motion he unceremoniously dropped the girl over his shoulder. She landed face-first in the sand, and he simultaneously took a roundhouse swing at one of the men. The man simply leaned back a few inches, and Alfred lost his balance and fell to the sand, at which point the two men set upon him.

Alfred awoke to a painful headache, and through squinting eyes, he assessed that he was bound to a large coconut tree. In a ring around the tree stood about twenty or more warriors, each held some weapon such as a short spear, war club, or long wooden club covered in shark teeth. He soon began shouting to get someone's attention so that he could be released back to his ship. No one seemed to pay him any heed, and he soon fell silent while trying without success to shield his eyes from the morning sun.

After more than two hours of baking in the sun, he watched as one of his shipmates, a tall, lanky fellow named Phillips, sauntered over and stood before him, temporarily blocking out the sun and giving him some immediate relief from its effects.

Phillips placed his hands behind his back and looked down, "You've done it now, Freddy boy."

"Done what?" Alfred spat out his reply.

"The girl you done grabbed up was the local chief's daughter and a member of the royal family. They call them the ali'i, and they got funny rules about touching them; it's taboo or something. Anyway, Captain's trying to negotiate your release."

Alfred added somberly, "I hardly remember what happened. Well, I'm sure the Captain will straighten this out."

Phillips continued somberly, "There's talk of a meeting with the Captain's daughter before the whole crew."

Alfred's head sagged as he contemplated his fate. The

Captain's daughter was a term for the cat-o-nine-tails, the whip used to mete out punishment aboard the ship. He had watched other men succumb to it, and even watching it brought hardened jack-tars to their knees and seeking God's forgiveness for their very own sins.

Phillips wandered off, and Alfred was left to agonize over his fate, and it did not take long for his agony to turn into a wave of self-righteous anger that welled up from deep inside of him. He would show them that he could not be hurt, that he was strong enough to withstand any arbitrary punishment they could hand out.

Phillips made a return visit some hours later, and Alfred lost any hope as he looked up at the grim look on the man's face. Phillips shook his head, "Captain done all he could, even offered to let the Chief come aboard the ship and watch you get punished ... but ... you broke one of their sacred laws called Kapu, and according to their law you have to die."

Alfred opened his mouth to speak but could find no words to say.

Phillips added, "Now they tell me that you got one chance to survive this thing. There are these Royal grounds where they have this sacred place of refuge, like a temple or something, and if you can make it there, well then they absolve you of your crime, and you're set free."

Alfred asked quietly, "So where is this place, and what's the catch?"

Phillips rubbed the side of his jaw and added, "Well, they got this wall that stretches all the way around the Royal grounds, supposed to be ten feet high and twenty feet thick. So first you gotta get over that, or you can swim in from the sea, but ... that way has lots of jagged volcanic rock and high waves and sharks, so that's probably out."

Alfred asked, "So once I'm over the wall, then what?"

"Then you have to ...," he paused, turned partway around,

and pointed at the warriors who still stood guard, "get past these fellas, I guess that's all there is to it."

An hour after that conversation, Alfred was released from the bonds that held him to the tree. In total silence, four of the warriors walked with him for some time through gently rolling fields of flowers and exotic plants, past high majestic waterfalls, and amongst a dense forest before stopping.

They stepped aside and motioned towards the forest. Alfred started walking slowly for a few moments before looking back; he saw no sign of the men. He then turned and began running for his life.

Fifteen minutes later, he exited from a thicket and stood facing a ten-foot-high wall of stone that had been pieced together without mortar more than three hundred years earlier. After a cursory glance to his left and right, he raced forward and leaped up and onto the wall. He pulled himself up so that he could just peek over the top edge of the wall. Seeing nothing out of the ordinary, he pulled himself up and onto the nearly twenty-foot long surface. He crawled along to the opposite edge and then dropped over the side, landing softly in the grass.

He moved forward, darting from tree to tree as he tried to remain hidden from any warrior who might be in this area. He was about to dash into a wide-open section of ground when a small spear embedded itself in the tree he was hiding behind. Alfred turned to see a warrior racing directly at him while waving a war club in a circular motion above his head.

Sprinting as fast as his legs would carry him, Alfred made it through the open space and entered into a thickly forested area where he skidded to a stop and pressed up against a large tree. The warrior chasing him never saw his prey until the branch that Alfred swung hit him across the face as he raced past the tree. Alfred quickly grabbed the war club and raced off into the jungle.

A few minutes later, he almost ran into another of the men hunting him. They faced each other for a second and then ran directly at each other. This warrior carried a long club with a flat surface that was studded with sharks' teeth, and both men swung their war clubs at each other with deadly force. The clubs struck together, and the shark teeth sprayed in all directions as the warriors' club shattered, and both combatants tumbled to the ground.

Alfred jumped to his feet, still holding the war club, looked down at the man lying on the ground moaning and bleeding, and raised the club over the man. Breathing heavily, he lowered the club and raced back into the wooded area.

Twice more, he came across these men who searched for him, and each time he was victorious in combat, leaving one man unconscious and one man most undoubtedly dead.

He stopped, taking a refreshing sip of water from a stream fed from a waterfall that dropped a hundred feet or more when he saw another warrior come from the woods and enter the stream less than one hundred yards away.

Alfred began yet another race for his life, pursued across a field of high grasses when he saw a second and third warrior enter the field from opposite sides. He leaped over a smaller stone wall and ran past a large wooden carved Tiki God statue. He climbed up onto a square platform that ran nearly twenty feet in each direction and turned to face his three opponents. Trying to catch his breath, he waved them forward with one hand as he held the bloodied war club up with the other.

The men pressed forward, approaching him on three sides. He then saw others emerging from all directions, and his arms came down to his sides, and he dropped the war club gently at his feet. Alfred closed his eyes and awaited the blow that would end his life.

Instead, he heard the beating of drums and the chanting of priests who circled him amid smoke and fire. He stood still as they anointed him with fragrant oils and made offerings of food and drink. He believed this was just a ceremonial rite that would be a prelude to taking his life and a sense of serenity fell over him.

He was soon taken by the hand and led from the Royal grounds and allowed to return to his ship, which remained sitting upon the bay's becalmed waters. Alfred returned to the vessel and was silently welcomed aboard by the Captain and the entire crew who looked upon him as Lazarus returned from death. There would be no flogging or further punishment meted out to him for his indiscretion, and on the following day, they would weigh anchor and sail off to continue their journey.

Alfred passed on his daily ration of rum or grog and indeed never touched such as that again for the remainder of his days at sea. His violent temper seemed to have been left on a distant shore, and it appeared that the blackness that had covered his mind had been washed overboard and allowed to sink into the depths of Davy Jones's locker.

Some years later, he left the sailor's life behind him and settled down in a harbor town where he lived in a house that overlooked the ocean. Here he spent his days helping craft small boats for fishermen and pleasure seekers alike. He married a widowed woman, and the two settled into a comforting relationship while showing many kindnesses to each other. Alfred became known for his pleasant disposition and occasionally sharing tales of a life of adventure upon the seven seas.

Alfred died peacefully in his sleep in 1901 at the age of seventy-one, and his last request was for a burial at sea.

"HISTORY IS A BATH OF BLOOD."

WILLIAM JAMES

BLAIR COUNTY
PENNSYLVANIA 1864
JOHN AUSTIN CARMACK, A DESCENDANT OF MADELINE CARMACK, A DESCENDANT OF RODNAN MACCORMAC

Along with his wife Mary and their four children, John Carmack lived a quiet life as a carpenter near Martha's Furnace in Blair County, Pennsylvania. They had already lost one daughter at the age of two, and their youngest daughter would not live to see one year. John, now thirty-five years old, stood about five feet six inches tall with dark hair and penetrating brown eyes.

The entire family stood outside their home and gazed off into the distance as the sky lit up, and the rumble of cannon could be heard. For nearly three years, the war that had been raging now saw the rebel Southern Army driving deep into Pennsylvania. His brothers Daniel and Henry had also served in the union army, and both died within two months of each other in 1862. Daniel died near Murfreesboro, Tennessee and Henry fell in the fighting during the battle of Perryville, Ohio.

John stated, "When war gets so close to home that you can hear the cannon, it's time for every man to join up."

On a bitterly cold and snowy day in early February of 1864, John enlisted in Company 1, 55th Regiment of the Pennsylvania Volunteers. For the better part of three months, they marched and drilled relentlessly until they were assigned to 3rd Division, 10th Corps, Army of St. James.

They were then transported up the James River, landing on a peninsula between the Appomattox and the James rivers. They joined in attacks on rebel forces in Petersburg and then Richmond, where newly reinforced southern troops forced the Yankees to fall back.

The 55th was reassigned to support the Army of the Potomac. They moved down the James and then up the York before landing at West Point. They marched past the White House as John stared, hoping to get a glimpse of President Lincoln himself.

The 55th marched straight on to Cold Harbor, and on the first of June, they were thrown into battle where they captured a large number of confederate soldiers.

John was shocked to find so many of the rebel soldiers were either young boys or old men, all seemed gaunt, and about a third had no shoes. The battle continued for three days until a stalemate was achieved due to so many officers being dead or wounded that both sides withdrew.

Skirmishes continued until the night of the 12th: the 55th Regiment manned the front lines as all the other Union forces withdrew. John and his mates could only hope that the rebel forces would not attack, for there would be no reinforcements to come to their aid. Fortunately, no attack was forthcoming, and John and the 55th were able to withdraw safely.

They moved back to Washington and once more passed the White House as a ripple went through their marching formation, causing them to slow to a crawl. President Lincoln walked alone through their ranks, shaking hands, patting backs, and speaking quietly with many men. John could scarcely believe his eyes when Mr. Lincoln stopped and shook his hand.

The President asked, "What's your name, sir?"

"John Carmack, Mr. President."

"Do you have children, John?"

"Yes sir, two boys and two girls."

The President beamed, "Wonderful, give them my best."

With that, the President moved on down the line, and John fell back in step with the other troops.

Early on the 15th, they arrived at Petersburg and were thrown into fierce combat with the well-entrenched Rebel forces, both sides taking heavy losses. By the following day, some sixty-two thousand Union troops faced off against forty-two thousand dug-in rebels.

On the 16th, John rose to fire when a rebel musket ball struck him in the thigh. Shortly thereafter, John was carried off to the medical tents, but it would be hours before the lead ball was pulled from his leg after a rag soaked in chloroform was held over his nose and mouth.

As John lay on the bare ground recovering among hundreds of other wounded soldiers, a commotion arose. Gettysburg hero Joshua Lawrence Chamberlain was brought in, and while thought to be mortally wounded, he would ultimately survive. Later the 1st Maine Heavy Artillery Regiment would make a valiant charge with nine hundred men, during which they would lose six hundred and thirty-two of their number.

A feverish John was moved twice more that day as other wounded constantly arrived needing assistance and as the battlefields' movement dictated. Over the next four months, John was moved numerous times during which his wound became infected, and he slipped into and out of a feverish state. One-stop found him lying among wounded soldiers suffering from dysentery, and at another, he lay among wounded rebel soldiers for several days.

By October 8th, John suffering from severe diarrhea and exhaustion was admitted to McDougall General Hospital in Fort Schuyler, located in Throg's Neck in the city of New York.

On the evening of October 25th, 1864, as Mary Carmack was putting the children to bed, she heard John call out her name twice. She quickly gathered the children, and they raced to the door, flinging it open in excitement to see their father. They found no one was there or received any answer to their calls.

Weeks later, Mary received notice of John's death on the night of the 25th of October. The nurse and doctor stated that she could take comfort in knowing that just before John died, he had sat up in bed and called out her name twice.

After the war, Mary would apply for and receive a pension of twelve dollars a month, which she would continue collecting until her death some forty-five years later. She would never remarry after losing her husband of eleven years in the war.

"IT WAS NOT WELL TO DRIVE MEN
INTO FINAL CORNERS; AT THOSE
MOMENTS, THEY COULD ALL
DEVELOP TEETH AND CLAWS."

STEPHEN CRANE, THE RED BADGE OF COURAGE

OKLAHOMA LAND RUSH 1893
ADAM MACCORMAC, SON OF EDWARD,
A DESCENDANT OF RONAN

Adam MacCormac was born in South Africa and was just nine when his father Edward, now wealthy from the diamond mining business, booked them passage to Ireland, the land of his birth. Adam had never known his mother as she had died during his birth and his father rarely brought up the subject; thus, he felt little attachment to the land of his origin.

His father found little to keep them in Ireland, and they made their way to America and the great city of New York. He settled with his young son into a nice hotel on the island of Manhattan, just one block away from the newly created Central Park. Adam spent many days playing and exploring there as it was then mostly used by the upper and wealthy class of society. His father invested his money wisely and even increased his holdings over time, yet was frugal when it came to daily expenditures or anything that would be considered mollycoddling his son.

Adam learned to make his way and often took odd jobs to earn his own money and impress his father with his industriousness. He refused even a token sum that his father wished to pay him for doing his assigned chores. This brought a smile to his father, which was worth more to Adam than any money.

The years slipped past, and now at twenty-two, Adam had fifteen men working for him. They delivered goods offloaded from ships in the harbor and then dispersed them all around the city. His business was thriving when one day in October of 1885, an ornate carriage pulled up in front of his cramped office. Adam was startled when his father jumped down, raced over, threw his arms around him, and lifted him into the air.

"My brother," he shouted, "Your uncle," it was all he could say as tears streamed down his cheeks. Adam had never seen his father cry and had no idea what was meant by the cryptic references to brothers and uncles as he urged his father to take a seat.

He went along with his father and sat in mostly silent contemplation as he listened to his father and his newly found uncle tell each other their personal stories. The stories told of their brothers and sisters' death, their parents dying, and their similar tales detailing their very kidnapping and subterfuge involved in their removal to France and South Africa. They also wondered what had become of their younger brother James.

Adam had no knowledge of the life his father had led and listened with new and profound respect as these two brothers shared their unique experiences. Over the next several years, the brothers alternated, one year, Edward would go to Paris and stay with his brother Robert and his family for a month or two, and the next year Robert would bring his family to New York.

Adam stayed active with various businesses; he came close to becoming very rich a couple of times and also lost everything on a couple of occasions. He met a headstrong woman named Sarah who was supervising the unloading of a ship owned by her father, and he immediately fell in love. She was used to the amorous looks, and rough language tossed around so easily down by the docks and refused Adams' advances. Still, he persisted, and after a yearlong courtship, they were wed.

He held his infant son in his lap when he saw something that would forever change his life. His eyes grew wide as he read about the fifth planned Land Run to be held out in the Oklahoma Territory in 1893. The newspaper article stated that millions of acres had been given away to any man or woman with the guts and determination to stake their claim over the past years. In 1889 over fifty thousand people raced to claim some two million acres. Stories told of those who had come to these lands with little to their name but now could claim ownership of their own land, their own homesteads. Each man could claim one hundred and sixty acres for him and his family.

He and Sarah talked of making a new start in a new land far away from their fathers' wealth, where they could become successful by their own hands and prove what they were made of.

Adam began liquidating his current assets and prepared to go to Oklahoma and get in on the great Land Run to take place in what was known as the Cherokee Strip. He found out that he could outfit himself and his family with the needed supplies in St. Louis or Kansas City, so that became his plan. His father was still in France on one of his visits, and Adam wrote to him and explained that he would go out west to claim his land and help build something new. Further, he told his father that once settled in; he would extend a formal invitation for him to visit the MacCormac Estate.

Adam had acquired a list of supplies from a newspaper that he might need to make the land run and another more extensive list required to build a home and all that that would entail. In St. Louis, he gave up after visits with three shopkeepers who had already sold out of any supplies he might need and only laughed when he asked when they might get more of the items in stock.

Adam looked out the window as he held his son on his lap, Sarah now six months pregnant, slept beside them as they journeyed to Kansas City via a train overloaded with people heading to the Territory to get in on the rush. Once in Kansas

City, he finally began to find items on his list, although at what he knew to be exorbitant prices. He purchased a team of four horses hooked up to an empty buckboard and then started filling it with food and sundry supplies. They then joined a train of more than two hundred wagons, buggies, and carts, all heading to Wichita and from there to the Kansas-Oklahoma Territory border.

On the first day of September, they arrived to find a burgeoning tent city that was a patchwork quilt with no rhyme or reason to it. Adam would wait in line for five days at the booth that served as one of only nine registration points for the run. He was one of the one hundred and fifteen thousand individuals who handed over their fourteen dollar registration fee. The requirements to register were to be a citizen, be over the age of twenty-one, and be the head of the household. It was mostly men who registered, although a few hearty women who were widows also did so.

It was estimated that counting in family members, there were about one hundred and fifty thousand people stretched for miles in all directions on September 9, 1893, and waiting for the signal to start the great Oklahoma Land Rush.

Adam had chosen his best horse for his solo ride, and he joined in along the solid line of horses and mules hitched to wagons of every description, shape, and size, and even the odd bicycle or two. The animals stamped and snorted and brayed as tension-filled both men and beasts.

At noon a cannon blast sounded, and this unleashed the stampede of land rushers forever to be known as Boomers as if they were one single entity in motion. Adam spurred his horse, imploring it to move beyond the tumult of humanity, all racing to reach the front of the line. His mind became numb to any thought other than getting the perfect piece of land upon which he could build a home for his growing family.

Nearly an hour later, he came to a valley filled with lush green grass; a clear stream of water meandered lazily through this section of land. Adam leaped from his horse and shouted to the heavens that this was now his land. As Adam looked around and began dreaming of where to build their home and plant their fields, a rather large and burly man rode up, telling him to get off this land as he had already claimed it. He accused Adam of being a Sooner, who had snuck in ahead of time to claim the land falsely.

As they stood yelling at each other, a third man came in, and he too claimed the land as his own. Within another ten minutes, there were four men all claiming this one plot of land. Adam watched in dismay as two of the men rolled through the dirt, grappling with each other. After several minutes of struggle, the man on the losing end sullenly wiped the blood from his nose, mounted his horse, and rode off. As the victor of this scuffle brushed dirt and dust from his clothes, the young man beside Adam decided this piece of land wasn't worth a fight and jumped on his horse and raced away.

The large man placed his hat upon his head, spat onto the ground, and said, "Time for you to move on too, sonny-boy."

Adam took two steps forward and replied, "I was here first, and this is my land now." Now just shy of thirty years of age, Adam added blithely, "And I'm no boy."

The man laughed, "First?" He waved his arm in a wide sweep, "Who's to say who was first? It will be my word against yours, and I can assure you that I am known to the authorities as an honest man. Who are you? Some no account drifter? Be gone with you sir, before I allow my anger to get the best of me and give you the thrashing you deserve."

Adam took one more step forward while the other man raised his fists and spat on the ground once more. As the two men circled each other warily, Adam's mind drifted far away, and he thought of his father, pirated away and sold into slavery as a young boy. He thought of his father's struggle to not only gain his freedom but to become a wealthy man. Everything he had was acquired with blood, sweat, and tears. Adam smiled as the thought rolled like a wave through his mind that he was indeed his father's son, and he would not let anyone come between him and his destiny.

When the two men came to blows, Adam unleashed a volcanic pent up fury as he pummeled the interloper into unconsciousness. Adam dragged the man through the dirt before tossing him over his horse's saddle; he then slapped the horse to send him on his way.

Adam began placing logs into a square as the house outline he planned to build for his family. He brought Sarah and his son to stay on the land while he went off to stake his claim at one of the four claims offices.

As he filed his claim, he had to pay for the land, with prices ranging from one dollar to as much as two dollars and fifty cents per acre depending upon the land's quality. He gladly handed over three hundred and twenty dollars for his one hundred and sixty acres.

Six months later, with his home nearly completed and ready to sow his first crop, he received his official deed to the property. They were among less than thirty percent of the Boomers who had survived for the required six months, the rest having up and left in the face of the hardships before them.

Adam stayed and helped to build not only his own home but the small town that sprang up not far away. He became a respected and revered man throughout the territory and even served as the town mayor for several years.

"THERE IS NO HONEST MAN!
NOT ONE THAT CAN RESIST THE
ATTRACTION OF GOLD!"

—————

ARISTOPHANES

YUKON TERRITORY 1896
GEORGE WASHINGTON CARMACK, A DESCENDANT OF MADELINE CARMACK, A DESCENDANT OF RODNAN MACCORMAC

George Carmack was born in California in 1860 and grew up listening to his father tell stories of panning for gold during the great gold rush of 1849. Orphaned by age eleven, he spent his teenage years scrambling to survive and, at age twenty, joined the Marine Corps as much for a steady income as for the adventure. It didn't take long for him to realize that he chafed at having to obey orders and longed to be on his own again.

While serving on the ship USS Wachusett, he sailed into Juneau, Alaska in 1882, and while on shore leave, he listened to stories detailing the search for gold in the Alaskan interior. With his fathers' tales ringing in his head, he deserted and headed off in search of his fortune.

For three years, he moved around following the whispers of gold miners in various towns and camps. While searching for his fortune, he found a coal deposit in what would later become named Carmack's city in the Yukon Territory.

In Juneau, he set about acquiring supplies to go prospecting once more. It would take him fourteen round trips over the treacherous Chilkoot Pass, the nearly one thousand foot trail that was the most straightforward route into the interior. On each trip, he carried almost one hundred pounds of supplies on his back.

Months later, he had settled in the Klondike where due to his ability to speak various Indian dialects, he had married a Taglish chiefs' daughter named Kate, who soon gave him a child.

In August of 1896, George went salmon fishing at the Klondike River's mouth along with Kate, his friends Skookum Jim and Dawson Charlie. Prospector Robert Henderson happened along and told them to go south and try fishing on Rabbit Creek. They packed their gear and headed off, hoping for better fishing.

On August 17th. while camped beside Rabbit Creek, George went down to the river to clean up after dinner. Rinsing his plate at the water's edge, he spotted a gold nugget nearly an inch long.

George would be the first man to file a claim along this stretch of water that would soon be known worldwide as Bonanza Creek. The word that fist full's of gold were lying about just waiting to be picked up and fortunes lay waiting to be made caused one hundred thousand men from all over the world to head for the Yukon.

The fortune seekers headed to Seattle and other Pacific ports before heading north to Skagway and Dyea. The North-West Mounted Police set up stations that required men to haul one tons worth of supplies over the Chilkoot Pass before they would be allowed to proceed. They would cut stairs into the ice on the mountainside; these were called the Golden Stairs. Some had to make as many as forty roundtrips to get the provisions through the pass. Once over the pass with their supplies, they had to buy or build boats for the five hundred and sixty-mile journey by river to get to Bonanza Creek.

Thousands died on the trek, and most turned back; still,

thousands made it through only to find claims had already been filed for all the prime mining spots. Within two years, the claims had all but been played out and nearly abandoned. George had made more than a million dollars, and now a wealthy man, headed off to California with his wife, Kate.

By 1900 George had left Kate and the baby penniless and moved to Seattle, where he remarried. Here he worked various gold claims without success and bought and sold real estate. He continued searching for another elusive strike until his death in 1922 that perhaps fittingly occurred as he swung a pick at his latest claim site.

"WE PENETRATED DEEPER AND DEEPER INTO THE HEART OF DARKNESS."

JOSEPH CONRAD, THE HEART OF DARKNESS

ETAT INDEPENDENT DU CONGO 1896
JOHN MACCORMAC, SON OF FREDERICK, A DESCENDANT OF RONAN MACCORMAC

Frederick and Maggie MacCormac lived quiet simple lives in County Cork near the southern coast of Ireland when their first son, John MacCormac, was born in 1878. He would be the first of their eleven children.

John was only twelve when he first went to sea aboard local fishing boats. By sixteen, he was a seasoned hand on a whaling ship in the North Sea that sailed out of Glasgow, Scotland. At eighteen, he served on a merchant vessel steaming south along the coast of Africa when they were caught in a violent storm that damaged their rudder.

The ship was forced to limp into the port city of Boma in the Etat Independent du Congo or the Congo Free State under the rule of King Leopold of Belgium. Upon finding that replacement parts could not be had and a new shipment would not arrive for at least eight weeks, the crew, including John, were given partial payment of their wages. They were released from their service and allowed to seek employment on any other ships in port.

John and two of his mates headed along the waterfront, passing by large heavily guarded piles of ivory tusks and bales of raw rubber. These they ignored, for they had coins jingling in their pockets and sought out a place to quench their thirst for rum and ale and possibly the comforting arms of a comely wench or two.

Four hours later, as they sat bleary-eyed but happy, they took no notice of the tall man in full dress uniform festooned with medals that stood near the bar and casually surveyed the men in the room. The man approached the three young seamen and stood over their table while twirling the ends of his long curled mustache until he had their attention.

He announced that he was a captain in the Force Publique that ruled over the Congo Free State and that good men were needed to serve in private companies in the countries interior. He stated that bonuses would be paid for meeting various production quotas in the collection of rubber and various other items. An industrious fellow could make more money in one year than he could in ten years at sea.

John rose unsteadily to his feet and, with effort, straightened up to his full height of six feet two inches and announced that he was not afraid of a little hard work and would gladly join up. His companions tried to convince him to stay, but his mind was made up, and they said their goodbyes. John picked up his duffel bag, slung it over his shoulder, and followed the captain out into the blinding sunlight and the oppressive heat.

By boat, they crossed over to the south side of the Congo River to the town of Matidi. Here John squinted mightily as he signed some papers written in Dutch and some in French, neither of which he understood. He stood before the blue flag with a gold star that was the Congo Free State flag and saluted. After some congratulatory handshakes, he was led off to dinner and given a cot to sleep in, and was told that they would leave in the morning for the interior. He drifted off to sleep with visions of the riches he would soon acquire and the stories he would tell the other lads someday.

In the morning, he ate his morning meal with six other recruits, after which they were issued a modified Stanley hat made with a white cloth that hung down on the sides and back to keep the sun off the tender skin of the white men. The hat was named after the famed African explorer Henry Morton Stanley. He had famously entered the continent's unexplored interior a quarter of a century earlier in search of Dr. Livingstone. He later went to work for King Leopold here in the Congo. The men were also given uniforms, repeating rifles, razor-sharp machetes, and a chicotte. The chicotte was a short whip made of dried hippo hide twisted at the ends and was used as the most effective means of motivation for the native porters.

John refused the chicotte, stating that the rifle and the machete were all that he needed. During his years at sea, he had seen too many men flogged with the all too similar cat-o-nine-tails. These mostly young sailors who had committed only some minor offense and were given the lash were never quite the same afterward, for the barbarity of the whip seemed to break the soul of the men just as much as it did their skin.

He had only fired a musket loader rifle once while onboard a whaling vessel. Still, he assured his new employer that he was experienced using the more modern repeating rifle. Each man was issued ten of the quick loading waterproof brass cartridges and told that they would be held to a strict accounting of each. They were under orders not to use them for hunting game or shooting any animals as their use was only for suppressing the natives.

They began their one to two months march to the interior along a narrow path hacked out of the jungle by those who had come before them. This long trek from the coast was necessary due to the Congo's nearly two hundred miles of impassable rapids that forced them overland. They soon caught up to the group's main body heading to the many military and trading outposts. This consisted of two Belgian officers, two white sergeants, twenty African soldiers armed with only machetes, and the ever-present chicotte. They marched alongside nearly three hundred porters, each of whom carried heavy loads of supplies.

John stared at the porters, each chained at the neck as he passed by them. All were men or boys either naked or wearing only small sections of cloth around their waists. All of them were emaciated, with rib bones showing through the skin. Their faces showed no emotion other than the sense of hopelessness to be gleaned from the blank, lifeless look of their eyes. What struck John the most was the scars of which many were bleeding, which covered nearly every one of the porters from the backs of the legs up to the shoulder.

John stopped as he saw one of the African soldiers using the chicotte on a man struggling to stay in step with the man ahead. The man dropped his load and curled up on the ground while screaming in pain. The column ground to a halt as one of the sergeants approached John and placed an arm around his shoulder.

"Don't worry about it lad. These natives are just dumb beasts, nothing more than lazy, ignorant savages who have to learn the value of work. It's up to us to motivate them to work. It's for their own good." The man laughed and shouted for the line to move out.

In the weeks to come, John observed any number of the porters drop from exhaustion. Some were struck with the butt of rifles until they were dead, others whipped until death was a certainty, and they would be left to die beside the trail or to crawl off into the bush. Two of the African soldiers and one of the recruits became sick with fevers and died within two days.

John became numb to his new surroundings and longed for the simple life of a sailor.

Finally, they reached a town now named Leopoldville after their Sovereign ruler that sat at the edge of a body of water called Stanley Pool, again named for the famed explorer. From here, John and the remaining recruits would travel on the Congo River by way of a steamer that had been carried here in pieces on the backs of porters. The jungle seemed immense and crowded the banks of the mighty river with a thick blanket of living things that appeared to mock the men's presence as insignificant. John sensed that they were always being watched as they moved slowly upriver through the air that at times seemed so thick that one could grab handfuls of it. Often, the morning's fog would slow their movements to a crawl as they navigated through shallows, sand bars, and rocks that could damage the hull and doom them to attempt escape by swimming to the river's edge.

Vast herds of hippos often made aggressive moves towards the ship if it passed them too closely, and large groups of crocodiles lined the banks or cruised on the surface, seeming to follow them at times.

The ship's captain warned them early on in their voyage not to fall overboard as the chances for survival were slim. This was demonstrated to full effect when one of the malnourished porters was found to have died during the night, and John and another man was instructed to throw the body over the side. John was surprised by the lightness of the body as they swung it out into the water. As soon as the body made contact with the water, the crocodiles on both sides of the river came to life and slithered beneath the surface. The boat had gone less than fifty meters when the water near the body erupted as if in a raging boil as the primeval beasts battled for their meal. John stared at the spot until they rounded a bend in the river, at which point John moved back away from the ship's railing.

The steamer passed villages with their primitive huts burned to the ground and others empty and now abandoned, seemingly left waiting for the jungle to reclaim them. When they did come upon an occupied village, it was with but a few women and small children.

A shout went out as they approached a trading outpost where one of the recruits was to be stationed. A few barely clothed African soldiers stood along the shoreline awaiting their arrival. In the background were one large whitewashed house-like structure with a white picket fence around it, there were two small huts to its left, and further back were three tents surrounded by another fence made from tree limbs. A few pigs and chickens were also enclosed within a small plot.

In front of the white house was a man sitting at a table writing in a ledger book. He took no notice of their arrival. He wore white pants, a starched white shirt with a collar, and a tie. A white linen jacket hung on the back of his chair.

John formed up with the others, and in a group, they began walking up to the house as the captain of the boat supervised the soldiers unloading supplies from the steamer's cargo hold. John froze in his tracks as they neared the fence, for atop each of the posts was a severed head, their faces contorted in agony and torment.

At the table, the man stood up and slowly put on his jacket, brushed his lapels, and picked a piece of dirt off of one sleeve before walking over to greet his new arrivals with a firm, authoritative handshake. Noticing John's apprehension, he said, "That's just to show these savages who's in charge here and let them know the penalty for disobedience." He slapped John on the back, "Spare the rod and spoil the child, and they're all like children without a meaningful thought in their heads."

John couldn't wait to return to the boat and resume the journey up the river. He sat quietly and tried not to imagine what horrors lie ahead. They stopped at two Force Publique military outposts to drop off supplies, each time John went below deck to his cabin and stayed there until they were underway again.

After three weeks on the river, they reached the outpost where John, now given the sergeant's rank, was to be stationed. He would be one of three white men at the post that twenty African soldiers also manned. Their sole mission was in the collection of rubber. After one day of rest, John joined the men as they went out into the jungle, trekking for hours until they reached a small village.

As they neared the village, all of the men ran off into the thickest of the forest, leaving only a few women and small children behind. The soldiers split into two groups, half headed off after the men, the others including John, rounded up those left behind. John watched as infant children were torn from their mother's grasp and thrown to the ground. The women who resisted were held down and had their right hands hacked off with machetes. The men hiding in the woods were quickly rounded up and brought back to the village for inspection. The oldest and weakest were beaten with rifle butts until they died, and then their right hands were chopped off.

With their families as hostages, the remaining men were taken deeper into the forest until they found rubber trees. Each man was given a quota of three to four kilos of rubber per fortnight; any who did not produce that amount or refused the task faced either their death along with that of their families or the loss of their heads and hands.

The rubber trees were one foot thick at the trunk with vines that coiled around them and their branches. The men would cut into the vines and allow the sap to drip into buckets. The men would then cover themselves with the sap in order for it to dry. Once dry, it would be painfully peeled from their skin, and then the process would be repeated again and again until it was too dark to continue.

On days when the rubber was brought in to be weighed, John fell into a deep depression, for he knew that any man who brought in a bale that didn't make the required weight would be killed most brutally and always in front of the other captives. On this day, the soldiers would also be awarded their bonuses, and John as a sergeant was to be given a portion of all his men's bonuses. A bonus was awarded for meeting the rubber quotas, for conscripts rounded up and for each right hand turned in. Basket after basket was brought forward, each filled with dozens of hands that had been smoked over fires to preserve them until collection day.

The troops moved from village to village, gathering males to be turned over as conscripts for the labor force. The soldiers were paid bonuses for each new conscript delivered. Other captives were used as porters. Chained neck to neck in groups from ten to twenty, they carried the raw bales of rubber to collection points where it could then be shipped back upriver.

John led a group of nearly one hundred porters to a remote outpost where they had to navigate several deep gorges via narrow logs used as footbridges. He watched helplessly as one man slipped off the log and pulled the other ten men chained to him to their deaths on the rocks far below. John stared down at them and thought that they were the lucky ones now safe from the terrors of life here in this land forsaken by God. The toes of his boots protruded over the edge of the rock ledge, and he closed his eyes as he leaned forward and pictured in his mind the weightlessness of his fall.

One of the soldiers grabbed his shoulder and shouted some unintelligible words at him. He moved onward with the column of doomed men, but his thoughts lingered behind, staring down into the black abyss.

Several weeks later, he boarded a steamer heading back to Stanley Pool without comment, silently vowing to leave this place without delay. He stayed below deck and avoided any conversations. He feared sleep and the nightmares that came with it. He could barely stand to eat as his body seemed reluctant to continue fighting. In his weakened state, he contracted malaria and had to be carried by porters for a week along the trail.

When his fever broke, he shuffled along listlessly for weeks until he found himself back in the port city of Boma, where his adventure had begun. He had been discharged from his service in the Congo Free State, and he adamantly refused to take payment in any form for his time there. The officers laughed at the foolishness of his gesture and split his meager pay amongst them.

He walked down to the docks and signed on with the first outbound ship he could find. He did not ask where she was sailing to, satisfied only that they were leaving this place.

"A DAY OF BATTLE IS A DAY OF
HARVEST FOR THE DEVIL."

WILLIAM HOOKE

49

SOMME RIVER, FRANCE 1916
ALBERT MACCORMAC, SON OF FREDERICK, A DESCENDANT OF RONAN MACCORMAC

Albert Frederick MacCormac was the last of the eleven children born to Frederick and Maggie. They were happily surprised at his delivery on the first day of the new century after only two of their previous ten children had been boys. He had never even met several of his older siblings; they had left the family home before his birth. Four of the previous ten children had succumbed to various ailments and passed away. The girls in the family doted upon young Albert as he battled through bouts of strange fevers that came and went over several years.

His sisters told him stories of his elder brothers, John, a sailor who traveled the seven seas to faraway and exotic places, and Edward, who now lived in America. They read him tales of gallant knights fighting for King and country and filled his head with stories full of romance and adventure.

Late in his fourteenth year, he watched as young men went off to fight the Huns in World War I. He marched with a stick on his shoulder and dreamed of joining in the battle to save all of

Europe. He read the sample recruiting form filled out with the name of Thomas Atkins that caused all British soldiers to become known as Tommies.

On the day of his sixteenth birthday, he walked into the recruiting office and filled out the form to join the war. The officer in charge handed him back the paper and explained that he was too young to join, stating that he would have qualified if his birth date had been listed as 1898 instead of 1900. Albert took the form and returned to his seat, making the necessary adjustments before again handing it in. The same officer smiled as he stamped the form and sent him on for processing with a wink and a hearty handshake.

Soon issued a khaki-colored tunic, trousers, and steel helmet, he began learning how to shoot a Lee-Enfield rifle. Across the Channel and now on European soil, his battalion of one thousand men trudged alongside the muddy roads heading towards the front lines near the Somme River. A steady stream of medical ambulances headed away from the fighting, many were drawn by teams of horses, and all were filled with wounded and dying men.

Albert's unit was made up of men from all parts of Britain as early in the war many units had been made up of men from the same towns, called Pals Battalions. They were planned this way to keep up the morale of the men. When they went into battle, they were often killed en mass, and whole towns and villages were devastated by their loss, thus leading to their current more diversified makeup.

Still, several days away from the front, they watched in wonder as far off in the distance the skies lit up at night like a gigantic lightning storm that never ceased. They stood at attention as a column of cars sped past, supposedly Lord Kitchener and General Haig, the men leading the British Expeditionary Force, were reviewing their newest troops. The men cheered heartily as they passed. Many, if not most, would never live to hear that General Haig would become known as The Butcher of the Somme.

One day out, they became used to the sound of the artillery that never seemed to cease. Still, a constant stream of ambulance lorries passed by as a grim reminder of what lay ahead. The men ate a hearty meal of beef, potatoes, biscuits, and jam before the order was given to move out to the front.

As darkness fell, they headed into the communication trenches that had been dug nearly two years before by sepoys, the British Empire's troops from India. These led in a zig-zag pattern to the front line trenches. These were mostly two to three feet wide at the top and tapered down at the bottom, lined with branches and twigs otherwise known as wattle on the sides and boards along the bottom. There was just barely enough room to squeeze past the haggard-looking men already occupying some sections.

The trenches to the front had firing steps built-in and were topped on both sides with layers of sandbags, those facing the enemy lines to protect them from enemy fire and those facing the rear to protect against artillery bombardments that fell behind them. Quietly they took their positions, mixing in with troops already on station. Albert's stomach was in knots as they awaited the unknown. A soldier with mud splattered coat squatted down next to Albert and grinned, "Don't worry lad, this is a quiet area. No attacks in this sector."

As dawn broke, an enemy artillery barrage began, but the shells landed either in between the front lines or way behind them in open areas. The response from the allied artillery came quickly and just as suddenly ended. Albert watched without comment as the veteran men began firing their weapons high into the air without aiming toward the enemy. He could hear similar firing coming from the German positions. This went on for fifteen minutes, during which he joined in at the urging of others. Then silence settled in, and the men relaxed. His new friend gleefully explained, "Everybody fires off a few rounds, that keeps the generals happy as we continually request more ammunition and supplies, and we all get to live for another day."

Albert smiled but felt cheated out of his chance to teach the Huns a lesson and wondered if these men were nothing more than cowards hiding from the real fight. That night they dined on bully beef in tins along with biscuits and apple jam. Old petrol cans now filled with water and carried from the rear brought them no relief as the water tasted of the petrol they once were filled with. The veteran men could tell the brand of petrol by the taste of the water. At four in the morning, men came around with ceramic jugs issuing each man his daily ration of rum. He was told that the German soldiers received schnapps each day, and occasionally a trade could be had. Albert downed his rum and welcomed the warmth it provided.

Two weeks later, after endless days of rain, they were given orders to move out, and the relative peace and quiet were replaced with a mixture of excitement and dread at what lay ahead as they moved to an "active" section of the front. Constant shelling by the British eighteen pounders, French 75 mm howitzers, and mortars were answered in equal measure by the German 149 mm guns. These trenches were a mix of ones that had been in use for more than two years and others newly dug to replace sections that had suffered direct hits and collapsed. They were muddy and filled with water that lapped at their heels. Legs, arms, and skulls of the dead protruded from the sides of the freshly dug trenches, and the ground trembled as the shells impacted the land around them and showered them with bits of earth and rock.

Less than fifty feet from their trench, the razor and barbed wire began in seemingly endless ribbons. Shell holes pockmarked the dreaded no man's land between the lines. Rats roamed everywhere, feasting upon the bodies of the dead, making no distinction as to their nationality. Every man was also infested with lice, and after a short time, many men suffered from trench foot due to continually standing in the water that rose above the duckboards placed on the bottom. To move anywhere meant slogging through the thick clinging mud.

Albert was issued a trenching tool, a short-handled shovel, and assigned to burial detail. At night under cover of darkness, a team of six men followed a chaplain over the top and out to recover the bodies of the dead and prepare them for burial.

They moved carefully among the strings of wire from shell hole to shell hole, these were often filled with water, bodies, and various body parts and the ever-present rats gnawing on the remains. Shallow graves were dug, the bodies rolled in, and each man would place eight or ten shovels full of dirt over them as the chaplain said a brief prayer. Shells still fell sporadically among them, and snipers fired random rounds in the direction of any sounds detected. Hence, the burial parties often found themselves seeking cover upon the muddy ground.

The French were under heavy pressure at Verdun when the order for an attack on the Somme was given. For days on end, the artillery barrage never ceased night or day, and Albert had a ringing in his ears, and his hands twitched from the incessant barrage. Albert pulled out a sheet of paper and wrote to his mother.

"Dearest Mother, I am well and amongst a good group of lads as we prepare for an attack in the morning. I look forward to giving the Huns a good licking. Our officers have assured us that the Germans will be on the run. This assurance is unneeded as we who have witnessed this week's artillery attack are certain that no one could withstand such an impressive display of might. This battle may turn the tide and allow me to return to you soon. Your devoted Albert."

He tucked the letter into his breast pocket to send off after the coming attack. Albert had little appetite that morning as they prepared to go over the top. They placed their fingers in their ears as the final moments of the bombardment commenced. Two hundred and twenty thousand shells were fired at the German lines in just the last hour before the attack.

Albert followed his company sergeant major out of the trench along with tens of thousands of his fellow soldiers. They had only two hundred yards between their lines and those of the enemy as they marched side by side in neat rows. As the smoke cleared, they were surprised that even after days of constant artillery assault, the barbed wire seemed untouched and still an obstacle to be overcome. They advanced thirty yards before the German machine guns opened fire. The air felt heavy with so much steel passing through it. Shells fell all around them, and men disappeared from existence as the bombs landed among them. Albert dove into a shell crater as more shells exploded all around him. He was showered with dirt and mud and the shredded body parts of his comrades.

He lay curled up in as small of a ball as he could make until an officer pointed a pistol in his face and ordered him to continue forward. He moved onward into a withering onslaught of steel as men fell all around him. He crawled forward behind a protective wall of dead bodies and waited for a lull in the enemy fire that never came. Others rushed past him, and he closed his eyes and tried to picture his mother and his sisters, but his mind went blank.

A trio of soldiers dove to the ground beside him, each with looks of terror on their faces. Deep breathes were taken, and the four young men rose as one to continue their valiant charge. The men on either side of Albert tumbled backward, each man dead before he hit the ground. Amid the madness, Albert smiled as the vision of his mother came to him, just then at least two shells simultaneously landed amongst them.

When the smoke and dust cleared, there was no evidence of them remaining. They had been vaporized into thin air. Their mothers would weep for them and forever mourn their loss.

The British would suffer sixty thousand casualties before this day was finished and more than four hundred thousand during the four months that the battle of the Somme raged.

Maggie and Frederick received notice ten days later that their dear Albert was missing in action and presumed dead. Albert joined more than eight hundred thousand British subjects who would perish in the war that also left them with two million wounded.

The MacCormac family kept up hope that he had somehow survived as his body was never located to give them final proof of his loss. They wrote letters to the older brothers of whom Albert had never met and tried as best they could to deal with their grief. To their eldest son John they sent the letter to the last place they knew him to be, India. Two years earlier, he had sent a short letter stating that he was now a ship's captain sailing for the British East India Company. He was based in Bombay, India, and sailed a route back and forth from Constantinople. Their only other son was Edward, who had left for America in 1899 at the age of sixteen and now was a shopkeeper in Philadelphia with a family of his own.

Maggie kept a small shelf in her bedroom containing memories of her sons, each now far removed from her loving arms although always close to her heart. For the remainder of her years, she kept up the hope that Albert would one day walk through the door.

> "DEEP DOWN INSIDE, WE ALWAYS SEEK
> FOR OUR DEPARTED LOVED ONES."
>
> MUNIA KHAN

PHILADELPHIA,
PENNSYLVANIA 1918
EDWARD MACCORMAC, SON OF
FREDERICK, A DESCENDANT OF RONAN

Edward ate his breakfast while playing with his three children, and then he kissed them each in turn along with a gentle, loving hug for his wife, Susanna. Stepping to their apartment door, he paused and pulled a long white cloth from his pocket and carefully tied it around his face covering his mouth and nose before departing.

He walked briskly down the empty streets, amazed that they could be so deserted. Many of the shops were shuttered, schools closed, even the churches had canceled their worship services.

Reaching the street where his shop was located, Edward nodded to the few people he saw looking out from behind the safety of their windows. At the end of the block was the only business that seemed to be bustling with activity, and that was a mortuary.

People had begun dying three weeks earlier in small numbers, and the word was that dozens of people had mysteriously died yesterday throughout the city. The panic had been building, and the city's hospitals were overwhelmed with the flu cases, and many were turned away.

This so-called Spanish Flu had spread across the nation and worldwide so rapidly that officials were unsure what to do. People were told to stay in their homes and limit contact with anyone outside of their own family.

Edward kept the front door of the shop open, but no one came inside. In fact, only a small number of people even passed by. He was considering closing when Mr. Marston, the mortician, entered. He too had a cloth covering the bottom half of his face and stopped just inside the door. He held up a piece of paper and called out his order for various supplies without approaching Edward. He asked Edward to place the items outside and stated that he would have someone come by and pick them up.

Edward asked, "What's happening out there?"

The mortician removed his hat, pulled a handkerchief from his pocket, and began dabbing at the perspiration on his forehead. He shook his head slowly with a look of terror in his eyes as he spoke, "It starts with a sore throat, a fever, and headaches. The hospitals are turning people away lest their own staff fall ill." He paused and continued, "Young men, robust men, are healthy in the morning and dead by nightfall." He replaced his hat, turned, and hurried out the door glancing from side to side swiftly while he headed back down the street.

What few knew at the time was that several months earlier in March at Fort Riley, Kansas, some one hundred soldiers had fallen ill and many died. Doctors had no idea why this seemingly simple flu could kill strong fit men so quickly. The soldiers then dispersed across the country and to European battlefields carrying it with them. After Armistice Day in November, they returned home as the contagion began to rage.

No other business was done that day in his shop, and Edward headed home once more on the abandoned streets. Closing the door of their apartment, Edward quickly checked the children for any sign of fever and found none to his great relief.

During the night, his youngest began coughing, and by morning all three of the children were fevered. Susanna cradled the youngest in her arms as Edward tried to figure out what to do. Hearing voices outside, Edward opened his door and witnessed his neighbor clutching his crying children in his arms. The man turned and, with tears streaming down his face, plaintively cried out, "I took my Margaret to the hospital, but they turned us away. She died in my arms." Now with a look of fear, he shouted, "Bar your door and let no one enter."

Later that evening, both Edward and Susanna were coughing and fevered. The youngest child died in the night; their oldest son lasted for another day before he too breathed his last. Susanna rocked her remaining child in her arms until they both succumbed. Edward, now too weak to get out of bed and too overwhelmed with sadness to care, lay back, and slept his last.

Over three thousand miles away in County Cork, Ireland, Maggie MacCormac sighed heavily and sat down in front of a small shrine to her children. Her heart was heavy with the feeling that she had just lost one of her offspring, and she closed her eyes and prayed for their blessed souls.

Nearly one-third of the planet's population would suffer from the Influenza outbreak, and more than fifty million would perish before it ran its course.

"It's only when you're flying above it that you realize how incredible that the earth really is."

PHILLIPE PERRIN

PACIFIC THEATER WWII, 1941
ADAM MACCORMAC, SON OF
EDWARD, GRANDSON OF ADAM,
A DESCENDANT OF RONAN

Adam MacCormac was born in Oklahoma in 1921 to James and Suzanna and named after his grandfather. The latter had come to the Oklahoma Territory in 1893 to participate in the Great Land Rush. He was just six years old in 1927 when Charles Lindbergh made history with the first transatlantic flight from New York to Paris, France. That same year his imagination was forever captured as he was introduced to the sight of men who soared through the air. He sat on his grandfathers' shoulders as they cheered for these pioneers of the sky.

In each of the next two years, the barnstormers in their leather flying jackets and helmets, wearing goggles and white silk scarves, returned to their town, and each time he was mesmerized by their acrobatics and dreamed of joining them. His grandfather, who regularly regaled them with tales from both his and his father's adventures, encouraged him to follow wherever his dreams might lead.

By 1933 flying had become an all-consuming dream for him,

and he waited anxiously for the show to come to town. His grandfather now lay quietly in bed, his body failing but with his wits still about him. He called young Adam to his bedside and presented him with the three dollar fee that he would need for a ten-minute ride from one of the gypsy pilots who put on the shows that came to small towns all across the country.

Adam gladly paid his fee and eagerly climbed aboard while the pilot, who was only in his early twenties, grinned as he recalled his euphoria during his first flight not so many years earlier. The pilot wanted to give the young boy an experience to remember, and judging by the ear to ear grin that seemed permanently pasted on Adam's face after the flight; he had succeeded.

Two years later, Adam had joined up with a "Flying Circus" that like so many others, put on hundreds of shows each year. Eventually, his relentless desire and fearlessness led him to perform as a wing walker in the shows and from there to flying at the age of fifteen. He dreamed of setting distance records like the famed Lindbergh or perhaps speed records like Wiley Post or even to explore new places like Jimmie Angel, who had discovered the great falls in Venezuela that would forever bear his name. As another two years passed, Adam had become one of the best pilots and could imagine nothing better than to make a lifelong career out of flying. Over half a million passengers were now flying, and that number was growing by leaps and bounds every year.

Adam had just landed after an exhibition that included numerous loop-de-loops, barrel rolls, and several passes over the crowd while flying inverted when he was approached by the famed aviator Billy Mitchell.

Lt. Colonel Billy Mitchell had flown in World War One and had been an advocate for an Air Force separate from the other military branches. He would become known as the father of the modern Air Force. He talked to Adam about joining the cadet training program upon reaching eighteen, and that was all the encouragement he needed.

Three days after turning eighteen, Adam went to Randolph Field in San Antonio, Texas, to begin his training. After extensive medical exams, the men would be sorted into pilots, navigators, and bombardiers. His near-perfect eyesight allowed him to be assigned to the nine-week pre-flight ground school.

It was on to Primary Flying School, and this nine-week course included sixty hours of flight training, during which he impressed the instructors as a natural aviator. Then the graduates went to Basic Flying School, again nine weeks with seventy hours in the air. Here they learned to fly at night and with instruments and also went cross country. Decisions would then be made as to their assignments to either single or twin-engine planes.

Advanced Flying School came next with seventy hours in flight, learning aerial gunnery and combat maneuvers. Adam was now flying the single-engine AT6. Almost forty percent of pilots washed out of the training programs, and those who passed went on to two months of transition training in a specific plane before being deployed. Adam graduated at the top of his class as a second lieutenant and was assigned to the Pacific Theater.

Adam was first stationed in Hawaii at the naval base in Pearl Harbor, where he spent eighteen months before being sent to Manila in the Philippines. He was actually on leave in Australia when the Japanese launched their surprise attack on the Pacific fleet that lay at anchor in Pearl Harbor. The Japanese also attacked the Philippines, Guam, and Wake Island, among others, where in most cases, they caught them with their planes lined up in neat rows that made them easy targets.

Adam flew numerous missions in the early months of the war. He and the other American pilots were dangerously outnumbered by the Japanese Zeros and carefully picked their fights. Adam had two confirmed kills during aerial combat and saw several of his fellow pilots shot down around him during the dogfights.

He had one Zero pass by him trailing a thick cloud of smoke, and he circled back to add the coup de grace and send him to his final resting place. As his finger touched the trigger, he hesitated as the enemy pilot made no attempt at evasion and instead flew slow, straight, and steady. He pulled up alongside the Japanese pilot and could see him slumped over inside the blood-splattered cockpit. As he flew side by side, the young pilot raised his head, looked right at Adam, smiled, and nodded slightly before toppling forward, causing his plane to nosedive down into the water. That night Adam tossed and turned but could not find sleep as the face of the Japanese pilot haunted his memory.

After Manila's fall in March of 1942, the American pilots escaped to Australia and flew their missions out of Brisbane as the Japanese commenced attacks on the Australian mainland. Adam was assigned to the 17th Fighter Group flying the P-40E Warhawk. During this period, he shot down another Zero and was forced into a crash landing after making it back to base with only fumes remaining in his fuel tanks. His missions took him over Papua New Guinea, the Solomon Islands, the Caroline Islands, and dozens more.

Adam and five other pilots got involved in a dogfight with a dozen zeros at dusk as they flew over the island of Corregidor just outside of Manila Bay. At the outset of the attack, his plane was hit, and he struggled to maintain control while evading his pursuers. He had just passed over Lubang Island when smoke began pouring into the cockpit, and he knew his chances at making a run for it were doomed. Waiting until the last second, he bailed out at one thousand feet and watched from under the canopy of his parachute as his plane spiraled down into the waters of the South China Sea near the Mindoro Straits.

Darkness fell as he floated helplessly in the water, no longer able to see or hear any planes in the sky above him. He knew that his chances of making it to land were slim, and the Japanese would occupy any land he might be able to get to. That meant capture and, most likely, torture and death would be the result. The Japanese regularly sent patrol boats through the Straits and would more than likely shoot him as he floated in the water should they come upon him, so he made his peace with God and accepted his fate.

Fortunately, heavy clouds and a moonless night provided him with cover, and unbeknownst to Adam, one of his fellow pilots had seen him bail out and radioed his likely location back to their base. From there, the word was sent out, and the search for the downed pilot was on.

Ninety minutes later, Adam saw a small blinking light followed by voices speaking English. A submarine had been patrolling in the area when they received the alert; they surfaced and had begun searching for the American pilot at great risk. Adam was pulled into a small rubber raft by three grinning sailors who welcomed him aboard. Although distressed by his plane's loss and his resulting near-death experience, Adam felt rejuvenated when greeted on the sub with a rousing cheer. As the sub dove below the water's surface, Adam made his way throughout its stifling confines to personally shake the hand of every man on board. He could count himself among more than five hundred flyers that would be plucked from the oceans by submariners during the war.

He was taking a little R&R when he met the legendary Paul "Pappy" Gunn. The captain was forty years old, hence the title of Pappy to the young air force pilots. Pappy had served in the Navy during World War I as an aircraft mechanic before getting his wings; he later qualified as a naval aviator and flight instructor before retiring in 1939. He went to Hawaii and started an inter-island flight service later known as Hawaiian Air Lines; from there, he went on to start Philippine Air Lines. He was operating a civilian freight operation in the Philippines when the war started, and on the day after the attack on Pearl Harbor, he was sworn in as a Captain in the Air Corps.

Pappy would fly more missions than any other pilot during the war, and he flew them in numerous aircraft. Some of the craft he flew included the Beechcraft, DC 2's and DC 3's, B-17, B 25, and the A 20. He flew reconnaissance missions, transport of both men and supplies along with strafing and bombing missions. He was said to never fly above five hundred feet, preferring to hug the treetops when over the islands in the daytime or at night and almost touching the water when hopping between islands, all this in any kind of weather. Often he would land, refuel and load up with ammo and supplies and take off again to destinations unknown.

Pappy was shot down twice, once on the island of Cebu, and once on the island of Zamboanga; both times, he crashed in the jungle and spent weeks walking out and making his way back to safety. He landed his B 25 on the beach in the Philippines to pick up a Japanese double agent. He had won the Distinguished Flying Cross for flying an unarmed plane to bring relief supplies to the beleaguered troops on Bataan. He did all this even as his family was held captive by the Japanese after Manila's fall.

Adam enjoyed listening as Pappy spun tales of his many adventures to the other pilots, including one he told of making a sea landing upon the back of a whale where he then climbed out and stood on the whale while making engine repairs. The whale then supposedly slipped below the waves as he took off again.

During the Dutch East Indies campaign, Adam flew as the allies shot down forty-nine Japanese planes with a loss of only seventeen of their own. Adam later came down with Dengue Fever and spent time in an Aussie hospital while recovering. Adam became fond of the pretty blonde Australian nurse named Delores, who doted after him during his three-week stay. After several days he managed to get her to agree to go for dinner upon his release. He proposed to her the very next day, and he was over the moon with joy when she said yes.

He wrote to her every day that they were apart. It would

be three months before he got another leave, and they were married. She would be just one of the more than fifteen thousand Australian "War Brides" during the war.

Adam went back to flying fighter cover for the bombers with the latest innovation installed by Pappy. Pappy had directed the installation of four fifty caliber guns on all the A 20 Havoc light bombers, while on the B 25 Mitchell bombers, he added four fifty cals in the nose and two more on each side of the fuselage, and three more underneath. He joined in with one hundred and thirty bombers and fighters in the Battle of the Bismarck Sea, where they attacked a Japanese convoy sinking twenty ships and shooting down sixty planes.

During the attack, he was wounded in the left leg and left side of his chest. He would spend six weeks with Delores tending to his wounds before being shipped home to the states.

After the war, she would join other Australian women on "Bride Trains" that brought them to the states to reunite with their American husbands. They settled down in California near Santa Barbara and immediately joined millions of other GIs by starting a family that would eventually include five rambunctious boys.

Adam went to work for an airplane manufacturer and would fly small planes only on the weekends for pleasure. Occasionally he would take Delores and the boys up and show them what joy could be found in the skies. Once in a great while, when the mood struck just right, he would throw in a loop-de-loop or barrel roll just for fun.

"YOU GO THROUGH LIFE WONDERING
WHAT IT IS ALL ABOUT, BUT AT THE
END OF THE DAY, IT'S FAMILY."

ROD STEWART

SANTA BARBARA,
CALIFORNIA 1956
JOHN MACCORMAC, SON OF ADAM,
A DESCENDANT OF RONAN

John MacCormac was the last of five boys born to Adam and Delores MacCormac on Christmas day in 1956 at the tail end of the baby boom that had occurred after the Second World War. He was almost eleven when he picked up the phone two days before Christmas. It was his eldest brother Jack calling home from Viet Nam where he was serving in the Army.

Jack joyfully shouted, "Hey little brother, early happy birthday. Can you put Mom or Dad on, please?" John replied, "They're out Christmas shopping, and I'm here by myself. So are you killing any gooks, Jack?" Jack laughed, "Shut up, ya little punk. You just wait till I get home. I'm gonna box your ears." John quickly added, "I'm gonna join up and come over there and help you get them gooks." Jack shouted into the phone, "STOP IT; you don't know what you're talking about." After a long pause, he spoke softly, "It's not like that at all, little brother, you gotta stop talking like that... it's messed up over here... everything is fucked up."

John had never heard his brother swear before, although he

had heard the "F" word before. He heard Jack sigh heavily and say, "I'm sorry Johnny, I'm sorry... trust me, you don't want to come over here," and after a long pause, he added, "ever." He said quietly, "Tell Mom and Dad and your brothers I love them and merry Christmas. I'll be going out the next few days, so I won't be able to call them until after New Year's Day. I have another thirty-three days until I take the Freedom Flight home, and I'll see you then, Love you, Johnny." The phone clicked off, and John hung up the phone and cried, although he was unsure why.

On New Year's Eve, the family was just sitting down to dinner when the doorbell rang, and Mom said I'll get it and went to the front door. Her scream of the single word NO brought them all running. Two young men in military uniforms informed them of Jack's death two days after Christmas in the faraway jungles of Viet Nam. Their father, himself a decorated war hero in the Second World War, wrapped his arms around his wife as she sobbed uncontrollably, and their four remaining sons stood by with tears streaming down their faces.

Now just one month shy of turning seventeen, James ran to his bedroom and slammed the door. Jesse and Joseph solemnly went to the room they shared and closed their door softly as John fell across his mother's lap and joined her in grieving.

The day after Jack's funeral, the family sat around the table for dinner until their father stated, "James, you need to get your hair cut." James, whose hair hung down in curls at his collar, shouted back, "I won't cut my fucking hair." Their mother cried out, "Watch your language, young man." Their father stood up and slammed his fist on the table, "As long as you live in my house, you will obey my rules." James stormed from the table, went to his room, and slammed the door. Everyone ate in silence until the sound of James' stereo filled the dining room with the words of the musical group The Animals song, "I Gotta Get Outta This Place." Their father immediately went into the living room and put on his record of Sergeant Barry Sadler singing, "The Ballad of The Green Berets." The boys silently went to their rooms amid the disintegration of their family.

Despite the peace efforts of their mother, James packed up and moved in with friends. He would later enroll at Cal Berkeley and join in the antiwar movement, much to his father's chagrin.

John sat with his parents on December 1, 1969, and watched on television as the first of two draft lotteries were held. His mother breathed a sigh of relief as neither James nor Jesse had the numbers that corresponded with their birthdays called according to the chart listed in the newspaper. Even though James hadn't yet been drafted, he told his parents that he was opposed to the war, and if drafted, he would go to Canada before he would become part of Nixon's war. Despite his growing doubts about the war, his father stated that he would disown him if he did not do his duty to his country.

John, now thirteen, still played soldier in the backyard and tried to distance himself from the turmoil raging within his family. His brother Jesse spent every spare minute hanging out at the beach or in the water surfing, and Joseph banged away on a set of drums hoping to join in a band with some of the guys in the neighborhood.

In May of 1970, John sat with his parents as they watched in bewilderment at the news of kids being shot at Kent State University in Ohio. In the following days, nearly four million students would strike on more than four hundred colleges and universities across the country. James came home two weeks later to explain that he was going to Canada to evade the draft. His father quietly slipped him an envelope containing one thousand dollars, thereby expressing his growing discontent with the war. The family gathered together around the dinner table that night, unsure if or when they might all be united again. James would leave in the morning, and it would be another seven years before President Jimmy Carter pardoned all the draft resisters, and he would be able to come home without facing a five-year jail term.

It was the summer of 1971, and John sat in the living room with his parents as they watched the evening news while his father held the newspaper in his hands. The lead story was about the fallout from the Pentagon papers' release that detailed that the government had known the war was unwinnable, yet they still sent American boys into battle. John watched his father crumple up his paper and throw it to the floor in anger at the callous disregard shown to the young men who were forced into fighting and dying for a lost cause.

John came home from riding his bike to find a pounding racket coming from the garage. Jesse had joined a band with some guys from school, and they were practicing as John came in and sat down on the floor next to Jesse, who had just returned from the beach. John scrunched his shoulders as the vibrations echoed down his spine. The lead singer screamed unintelligible words while jumping up and down at a furious pace. Each band member seemed to be spiritedly playing a different song in a different key, although they all played at maximum volume levels.

The song ended, and with ringing ears, the band began high fiving each other at their own perceived awesomeness. John was getting up to leave when one of the guys handed him a hand-rolled cigarette. Jesse grabbed his arm and said, "Be cool, and don't say a word to Mom or Dad about this little Bro." He then added, "Just hold it in your lungs for a minute and mellow out." A little while later, as the band played on, Jesse leaned over to John and said with a laugh, "Joey's band sucks, but they got some great weed."

Joey and the band broke up a couple of months later, and he joined another band, and on the spur of the moment, they all piled in the bass players' beat-up van and headed out on the road to find fame and fortune. In Austin, Texas, while the band played, Joey spotted a pretty blonde girl in the crowd and instantly fell in love.

When the band moved on, Joey stayed behind with his new girlfriend. They moved into a small apartment where they would happily remain for the next several years until it became a little too cramped after their son's birth.

Jesse spent less and less time at his parents' house as when he did; there was always a hassle about him getting a job or cutting his hair or doing something with his life, so he generally tried to avoid the confrontations if he could. John came to see him once in a while at the beach house near Los Angeles that he shared with a dozen or more people, although no one seemed sure who owned it or how it was paid for.

The first time John came by, it looked as if it was the aftermath of an epic party. Still, subsequent visits showed it always looked that way, albeit with a continually changing cast of characters lying about in varying states of drug-induced slumber or hyperactivity. Jesse offered him a hit off a joint, and when John said he'd pass, his brother grinned at him, "Johnny, you're such a straight arrow Bro, you definitely take after the old man." John looked at his brother through a haze of smoke, "This just isn't my scene Jess." The boys hugged tightly and said goodbye.

Jesse got busted for possession of marijuana, and Joey, now seventeen, gave him some of the money he was saving for college to get out of that jam. Jesse would wind up in rehab twice before he straightened up and met a pretty girl while taking some classes at LA City College. They lived together for two years before he proposed, and he asked John to serve as his best man at the ceremony.

John was having dinner on a Friday night with his parents and noticed his father seemed very distant and melancholy. He smiled and asked his dad, "Say Pop, when are you gonna take me up flying again? We haven't gone in a while." As he had hoped, his father's mood brightened immediately, and they made plans to go up the next day.

Adam let his son take the controls as they soared through the air over the waters of the Pacific and then over the Santa Cruz and Santa Rosa Islands before heading back. John had flown with his dad many times and never felt closer to him than when they were together in the cockpit of a plane.

John was attending the University of California, Santa Barbara, that sat on cliffs overlooking the Pacific Ocean when he first saw the girl that would eventually become his wife. She was barely five feet tall and had jet black hair that hung straight down to the middle of her back. He was captivated first by her exotic looks and bright smile and then by her quick wit and keen mind. While he was an excellent student, she proved to be two steps ahead of him at every turn, and instead of being intimidated by her intellect, it inspired him. They had been dating for six months when he brought her home to meet his parents.

They walked into the living room, and his father stared at her with a blank but stone-faced expression that immediately sucked all the air out of the room. John looked from his father to his mother as his face turned red from anger. "This is Sondra Yamada, my girlfriend," he stated defiantly as Sondra tried to avoid his father's stare.

His mother smiled sweetly and took Sondra gently by the hand, and led her into the kitchen. John sat down heavily and said, "What the hell, dad? I mean, seriously, what's up with you?"

The anger boiling up inside him diminished a bit as he noticed tears welling up in his father's eyes. They sat in stony silence for several awkward moments before his father got up and took him by the arm and led him into the kitchen. His father asked everyone to please sit down, and John protectively took Sondra's hand in his own as they all looked at Adam.

"First off, let me apologize to you, Sondra, it's...," he paused, looked down at his hands folded tightly together and resting upon the table, and tried to compose his thoughts. "It's just ..... well, I .....," here he paused again and took a deep breath while slowly shaking his head. John looked over at his mother as she stared at her husband with a look of concern.

Adam looked up again and continued with a weak smile, "You see, I was a pilot in the war, a fighter pilot, and one time there was a Zero, a Japanese fighter plane that flew near me. He was trailing smoke, and I was going to go after him and shoot him down, but I saw that he was in trouble and ended up flying right up beside him. I could see him clearly in the cockpit, and I knew he was badly wounded. Anyway, he looked over at me, and I could see he was just a young guy, probably younger than you are now. So we looked at each other, and then he smiled and nodded at me. He then passed out, and his plane went down into the water. It's been thirty years since then, and never does a day go by that I haven't seen his face and wonder why him and not me, I wonder what would his life have been like if he had lived."

Delores looked over at her husband, who had never shared this with her, and she gently placed her hand over his. Adam continued, "So when I saw you, I could only see his face once more, and I was stunned. I'm sorry if I offended you."

Sondra got up and walked over to him as he stood up; she threw her arms around him and held him tight. Adam felt as if a weight had been lifted from his shoulders, and he hugged his wife and son as they shed tears of joy.

The remainder of the evening was filled with laughter and joy as they got to know each other. They shared stories about themselves and their families and dreamed of what the future might bring for them all.

Five years later, the lights on the Christmas tree twinkled as Adam and Delores welcomed everyone home. James was now home from Canada for the first time in seven years, and he brought his wife and two sons with him. Jesse and his wife brought their son and daughter in from their home in LA. Joseph drove in from Austin with his wife and their young son. John and Sondra arrived with their twin boys in tow. The house was filled with joyous bedlam and a wondrous love as they raised their glasses and toasted to the bright future of the MacCormac clan.

"WE CAN'T ALL BE HEROES BECAUSE
SOMEBODY HAS TO SIT ON THE
CURB AND CLAP AS THEY GO BY."

WILL ROGERS

POSTSCRIPT

My thoughts return again and again to all those ancestors across the ages that persevered through often unimaginable hardships. The challenges they faced daily to survive and indeed thrive were immense, yet here I am, the modern-day unwitting benefactor of their struggles and successes.

Among the challenges we know they faced was simply having their children live past the age of five, food production, gathering knowledge, the quest for exploration, and the ever-present shedding of blood in small battles and great wars.

Indeed, the infant mortality rate or surviving past the age of five was nearly fifty percent during much of the middle ages from 500-1500. That number did not go down much and was still forty-three percent in 1800 and thirty-six percent in 1900. As late as 1960, the rate still stood at just under twenty percent worldwide and is now under five percent in the twenty-first century. Data shows that in the United States in the year 1800, the average woman would bear seven children during her lifetime with only four surviving past the age of five. Today the averages are less than two children with a survival rate of ninety-nine point nine percent.

The need for daily sustenance would have been a significant obstacle, for if they did not grow crops for their own use, they would have been challenged to gather edible plants from the wild, to catch fish from local streams, rivers, lakes, or oceans, or trap and hunt wild game. The pain inflicted upon the heart of the parent of a child who cries out in hunger transcends the ages. The mother who would gladly postpone her own needs so that her child is cared for is true no matter what period we look at, no matter what continent or nation she lives in.

The quest for knowledge has often been thwarted as education was generally restricted to the church's ruling classes and representatives. Despite the general lack of educational opportunities and systemic illiteracy over the last thousand years, there have always been learned men who sought answers. Even now, as modern man has easy and immediate access to virtually all of humanity's recorded history, and illiteracy is fast being eradicated, we tend to think of ourselves as smarter than those who came before us.

How can we look upon a man such as Omar Khayyam, born in Persia nearly one thousand years ago who was a mathematician, scientist, astronomer, and philosopher and say that any man today could match or exceed the quality of his mind?

Can one study the life of Leonardo da Vinci and not concede the greatness of his mind. He was able to scientifically study the human body in such detail that he could document and describe the heart's inner workings and its functions and give an analysis of arteriosclerosis or hardening of the arteries that would not be confirmed by medical doctors for another five hundred years. Leonardo would also create some of humankind's most outstanding artistic achievements, such as the Last Supper and the Mona Lisa painting.

At the same time and in the same place as Leonardo da Vinci was yet another artist by the name of Michelangelo. His works include the statue of David, carved from a massive block of marble, and the painting of the ceiling of the Sistine Chapel, and they have awed any who have witnessed their magnificence. Could a modern man accomplish achievements that will be universally admired and endure as long, only time will tell?

From our beginnings as hunter-gatherers who roamed the land in search of sustenance, until man began cultivating crops and thus settling down into ever-larger communities, there has always been a sense of wanderlust in man's nature. Even during periods when people gathered together, and some portion of the worlds' population lived and died within a relatively short distance of where they were born, there were still some who sought to look over the next horizon. To find out what was over the next mountain or across the wide rivers and vast oceans. They had to overcome their fears of the unknown. Many, who left never returned, their families never would know their fate, could never be certain if they had found a better place to build a life or been swallowed up by the incalculable mysterious places to which they ventured.

The intrepid explorers set sail upon seas, not knowing whether they would sail off the edge of the world or not. They also set off on foot in groups large and small and sometimes as individuals. They set aside their trepidation and anxiety as they ventured into the possible domain of fearsome and mysterious beasts, monsters of the land and sea. They went with apprehension over the strange and possibly unfriendly people they might meet.

Still, they went in all directions of the compass. They found lands both barren and forbidding and fertile and promising. They came across exotic plants and animals of the land, sea, and air that astounded them. They met native peoples, some of whom were friendly and welcoming, and others who were fearful and hostile.

They traversed great inhospitable deserts, vast open plains, and dense impenetrable forests. They climbed mountains topped with ice and snow and rapidly flowing rivers teeming with dangerous wildlife. They planted their flags and created new settlements everywhere they went.

Some brave travelers perished from illness or injury; others lost their lives to the unrelenting cold or oppressive heat. Hurricanes or typhoons took many ships upon the high seas to a watery unmarked grave. The courageous explorers also lost their lives in violent confrontations with the indigenous peoples.

Unfortunately, any look back at the history of humanity will find one near-constant that shows up among all nations, all empires, among all races, creeds, or religions. That constant is conflict resulting in widespread destruction, warfare, and death.

We see the kingdoms of Ireland battling each other for supremacy, the Crusader knights fighting against Islamic forces for more than two hundred years, Genghis Khan and his Mongol armies sweeping over Asia, and Kublai Khan conquering China. The Scots united behind Robert the Bruce fighting for years as they strive for their independence from England. England and France engaged in an off and on again war that lasted one hundred years. Spanish explorers waged bloody conquests in the Caribbean and then into Central and South America, where the Incas fell victim to their lust for gold and treasures. Seafaring pirates violently preyed upon ships at sea, often with their government's sanctioned approval.

In America's colonies, settlers pushed westward into native Indian lands and provoked violent and deadly clashes. The colonists in America waged war for independence from England. During the conflict England armed the Indians and brought in Hessian troops while the colonials received assistance from the French. Half a century later, the British seeking to maintain and expand their Empire would send troops into Afghanistan for the first of three wars they would wage there.

The American nation would become divided between North and South in a bloody and deadly four-year struggle that would take more than six hundred thousand men's lives.

Two world wars would rage around the globe in bloody and deadly conflicts that would cause millions of deaths and untold devastation to millions more.

Our ancestors persevered through all of these challenges, both during periods when it may have seemed hopeless to continue because nothing appeared ever to change and opportunities were nonexistent and during times when they were forced to adapt to the whirlwind of constant changes in their lives. Our forbearers faced the dullness of unvarying daily tasks that pushed them physically and the excitement of stepping out into the unknown to confront their fears. They fought and died, lived and loved, and still, their legacy lived on. Each new generation continued to move forward, whether that would be inch by inch or by leaps and bounds.

So here I sit in a twenty-first-century life and look back in reverence upon all who have come before me. Most lived quiet, perhaps even dull lives, at least to our modern-day sensibilities. Most of their stories were never recorded or, if so, now have been lost to history. Indeed, it is true that the victors have most often recorded history, and thus the stories are slanted in their favor.

I can only use my imagination to bring them to life once more; from their rebirth on these pages, I honor their memory and their sacrifice, while you, the readers, and I stand as living proof of their very existence. We stand upon the shoulders of countless generations whose legacy will endure long after we have passed from this earth.

So it is in the same manner that an orphaned child given the name Angus Cormac would live his life in a most ordinary way leaving behind five sons who would each leave a legacy in his name that would reverberate throughout the ages.

Robert James Carmack

AUTHOR BIOGRAPHY

Robert James Carmack was born in Akron, Ohio and now resides in South Carolina. Clan Cormac was begun in January of 2014, put on the shelf for more than two and one-half years before being completed in 2019. This is his fifth book, and he hopes that you enjoy it. He can be reached via e-mail at bc2u56@ gmail.com.

NOTES, COMMENTS, AND FURTHER READING

In researching this book, I used numerous source materials, including many trips to the library, reading a large number of books on various subjects, and internet searches.

Of these, I would like to list just some of the many websites used:

Brainy Quotes
Goodreads
Ancient History Encyclopedia
Brittanica.com
ScienceMag.com
History Today
History.com
Hyperhistory.com
Wikipedia
AncientOrigins.net
Pioneers of Flight.edu
All Things Aviation.com
The Canadian Encyclopedia
Quotes from famous people.com
How Stuff Works
Eyewitness to History
New World Encyclopedia
Google Earth and Google Maps
Biography.com

Dochara.com – insider guide to Ireland
Rootsweb.com – Ireland's history in maps
CDC.gov
Baby-names of (Ireland, England, Scotland, France, Switzerland, Italy, Spain, Portugal, Australia)
Behind the Name
Project Guttenberg

A partial listing of books used as reference material:

The 2548 Best Things Anybody Ever Said by Robert Bryne, 1982.
Crusades, The Illustrated History by Thomas F. Madden, Editor, 2004.
One Bloody Thing After Another by Jacob F. Field, 2012.
Timelines of War by David Brownstone and Irene Franck, 1994.
The History Book by DK.com, 2016.
Where They Fell by Tim Newark, 2000.
Weapon – A Visual History of Arms and Armor by DK.com 2006.
King Leopold's Ghost by Adam Hochschild, 1998.
Heart of Darkness by Joseph Conrad, first published as a partial serial in Blackwood's Magazine in 1899.
Adventures of a Mountain Man by Zenas Leonard, 1839.
The Dark Ages 476-918 AD by Charles Oman, 1895.
World War I – The Definitive Visual History by DK.com, 2014.
Unknown Soldiers, The Story of the Missing of the First World War by Neil Hanson, 2005.
To End All Wars by Adam Hochschild, 2011.
Saga of Pappy Gunn by George C. Kennedy, 1959.
U.S.S. Seawolf: Submarine Raider of the Pacific by James David Horon, Jim Eckberg, and Gerald Frank, 1945.
Can Do! The Story of the Seabees by William Bradford Huie, 1944.
War In the Pacific: Out In the Boondocks U.S. Marines Tell Their Stories by James Horan, 2017.

Island of the Damned: A Marine At War in the Pacific by R.V. Burgin, 2010.

Leonardo Da Vinci by Walter Isaacson, 2017.

Life of Mungo Park in Africa by Mungo Park, 1799.

Travels In the Interior of Africa by Mungo Park, 1799.

The Decline and Fall of the British Empire 1781-1997 by Piers Brendon, 2007.

Reference specific to chapters as noted below:

The use of Brittanica.com, the Ancient History Encyclopedia, Biography.com, Wikipedia, History.com, to name a few, were used on multiple occasions and will not be listed separately with each chapter.

Chapter 1- Dochara.com, Rootsweb.com, Baby Names of Ireland.

Chapter 2 -The Mariners Museum and Park.org

Chapters 9-14 – Many sites and books relating to the Crusades, The Knights Templars, and The Knights Hospitaller.

Chapter 12 – History of Switzerland.com, Culturestrip.com

Chapter 13 – BBC.com

Chapter 15 – dailymail.com, all that's interesting.com

Chapter 17 - Leonardo Da Vinci by Walter Isaacson, 2017.

Chapter 36 – First Fleet.com

Chapter 37 - Life of Mungo Park in Africa by Mungo Park, 1799.

Chapter 40 – The Capetown Museum.org, sahistory.org

Chapter 43 – Poetry Foundation.org, History Extra.com, British Battles.com

Chapter 44 – Pu'uhonua O Honaunau National Park Service website.

Chapter 45 – Carmack Family History / Family Tree by Karen Carmack Stadler, 1994.

Chapter 46 – Oklahoma Historical Society.

Chapter 47 – Klondike Gold Rush.com, PBS.org

Chapter 48 - King Leopold's Ghost by Adam Hochschild, 1998.

Chapter 49 - Unknown Soldiers, The Story of the Missing of the First World War by Neil Hanson, 2005, To End All Wars by Adam Hochschild, 2011.
Chapter 50 – CDC.gov
Chapter 51 - Saga of Pappy Gunn by George C. Kennedy, 1959.

Author comments by chapter:

Chapter 1 – Cormac mac Cuilennian was a real man who was an Irish Bishop and later named as a King. His life and death are portrayed accurately.

Chapter 2 – The exploits of Erik the Red are accurately detailed here, although any fictional characters' interactions are conjured only from my imagination. Erik's second in command, Ragnall, is also a fictional construct. The details of the city of Constantinople are accurate.

Chapter 4 – Brian Boru, the first true King of Ireland, and his death's accounting is accurate per historical records.

Chapter 6 – Accounts of the Crusades are heavily documented and accurately portrayed here, albeit with fictional characters mixed in. The Crusader attack on the city of Constantinople is accurate. The accounting of the "Childs" Crusade is also taken from the historical record.

Chapter 7 – Genghis Khan and his Mongol army are accurately depicted.

Chapter 8 – Marco Polo's journey is well known and well documented, as was his meeting with Kublai Kahn in the city of Xanadu.

Chapter 9-11 – The Templars' story is well known and well documented, and my fictional characters are placed in historically accurate places and situations.

Chapter 12 – The actual story of William Tell has been much debated as to its accuracy. I have placed my fictional characters into an account of Tell's well-known tale.

Chapter 13 – My fictional characters interact with real-life Robert the Bruce, King of the Scots, in historically accurate settings.

Chapter 14 – The Black Death led to 75-200 million deaths or up to 60% of the population. It would take the world another 200 years to recover its population to the pre-plague numbers.

Chapter 15 – Bethlehem Hospital is used as a backdrop for my fictional characters. The patient "treatments" depicted were in actual use in Bedlam during its 400-year history.

Chapter 16 – I placed my fictional character into a place where she interacts with Joan of Arc after suffering a wound to her shoulder during the Hundred Years War. While the general details about Joan are accurate, her care by Winifred is not.

Chapter 18 – Details surrounding Leonardo Da Vinci and Michelangelo's lives are accurate except for their interactions with my fictional character Filippi.

Chapter 19 – My fictional characters join Christopher Columbus and Ponce De Leon in historically accurate depictions of their journeys to the New World. These include De Leon's search for the ever-elusive "Fountain of Youth."

Chapter 20 – My fictional character Miguel joins Ferdinand Magellan on his historic voyage and his ultimate death on the island of Mactan.

Chapter 21 – Tells of Francisco Pizarro and the conquest of the Incas. The details of their exploits are historically accurate.

Chapter 22 – This is a historically accurate portrait of life in Ireland and of the hardships posed to those who became indentured servants going to the new world.

Chapter 23 – My accounting of indentured servitude and slavery in the American colonies.

Chapter 24 – This tale was inspired by the "headright" system in Virginia that, among other things, allowed individuals to earn the rights to wilderness lands by building homesteads and clearing lands on the frontier.

Chapter 28 – Includes information based upon the life of William Woodward and the founding of Charles Town.

Chapter 31 – Inspired by the stories of Captain William Kidd and Edward Teach, also known as Blackbeard.

Chapter 32 – Includes an accounting of the Scot's Darien Scheme that planned an ill-fated expedition to build a settlement on the Isthmus of Panama.

Chapter 33-34 – A depiction of Irish immigrants joining in the fight for American independence from England and George Washington leading his troops across the Delaware River.

Chapter 35 – Inspired by the exploits of Daniel Boone.

Chapter 36 – The tale came from the story of the "First Fleet," which brought convicts from England to the newly discovered land of Australia.

Chapter 37 – Inspired by the real-life adventures of explorer Mungo Park in Africa.

Chapter 38 – An accounting of the British army's retreat from Kabul during the First Anglo-Afghan War.

Chapter 39 – My fictional characters caught up in the Great Famine in Ireland caused by the potato blight.

Chapter 40 – Taking inspiration from the discovery of the Eureka diamond in South Africa.

Chapter 41 – Inspired by Frederic Auguste Bartholdi's life and the construction of the Statue of Liberty.

Chapter 42 – My fictional retelling of the Australian Gold Rush.

Chapter 43 - A retelling of the famed "Charge of the Light Brigade."

Chapter 44 – Inspired by the story of the Great Wall of Kuakini on the island of Hawaii.

Chapter 45 – My real-life two times great-grandfather John Austin Carmack has his tale told here in my accounting. Although specific details are unknown, this story is historically accurate. He was not a relation to the book's fictional line of the Carmack or Cormac families. Genealogy research leads his actual lineage back to Evan Carmack, who served during the American War of Independence, and farther back to John Christopher Carmack Sr. who was born and died in Dublin, Ireland (1633-1710).

Chapter 46 – A fictionalized retelling of the Great Oklahoma Land Rush of 1893.

Chapter 47 – An accounting of George Washington Carmack's life and his discovery of gold in the Klondike. He was not a descendant of my fictional Carmack or Cormac families, nor is he related to my true Carmack lineage.

Chapter 48 – My accounting of life in the Congo Free State during the 1890s.

Chapter 49 – World War I was depicted by my fictional 16-year-old Albert and was inspired by the missing soldiers of "The War To End All Wars."

Chapter 50 – A fictionalized account of the Influenza epidemic of 1918.

Chapter 51 – World War II fighting in the Pacific Theater inspired by the brave men and women who fought there and featuring Pappy Gunn's exploits. This story also received inspiration from the early pioneers of aviation.

QUOTES USED IN THIS BOOK

Mark Twain - *"There was never yet an uninteresting life. Such a thing is an impossibility. Inside the dullest exterior, there is a drama, a comedy, and a tragedy."*

Irish Proverb - *"You've got to do your own growing, no matter how tall your grandfather was."*

Voltaire - *"Every man is guilty of all the good he did not do."*

Osage saying -*"If you want a place in the sun, you must leave the shade of the family tree."*

Harry S. Truman - *"There is nothing new in the world except the history we do not know."*

John W. Gardner - *"History never looks like history when you are living through it."*

Voltaire - *"It is forbidden to kill; therefore all murderers are punished unless they kill in large numbers and to the sound of trumpets."*

African Proverb - *"Until lions have their historians, tales of the hunt shall always glorify the hunters."*

Edgar Allen Poe - *"The scariest monsters are the ones that lurk within our souls."*

Robert Louis Stevenson - *"Everyday courage has few witnesses. But yours is no less noble because no drum beats for you or crowds shout your name."*

David Ebershoff - *"We are born, we live, and we disappear. One of the chilling aspects of history is the swiftness with which it carries us into oblivion."*

Dylan Thomas - *"Though lovers be lost, love shall not; And death shall have no dominion."*

William Shakespeare, Twelfth Night Act II Scene 5 - *"Be not afraid of greatness, some are born great, some achieve greatness, and some have greatness thrust upon them."*

Andre Gide - *"Man cannot discover new oceans unless he has the courage to lose sight of the shore."*

Ambrose Redmoon - *"Courage is not the absence of fear, but rather the judgment that something else is more important than fear."*

Julius Caesar - *"I came, I saw, I conquered."*

Antonio Porchia - *"Set out from any point. They are all alike. They all lead to a point of departure."*

Voltaire - *"It is dangerous to be right in matters where established men are wrong."*

Jules Verne – *"Anything you can imagine, you can make real."*

George R.R. Martin - *"When the sun has set, no candle can replace it."*

Robert Louis Stevenson – *"Don't judge each day by the harvest you reap but by the seeds you plant."*

Joseph Conrad - *"There is nothing more enticing, disenchanting, and enslaving than the life at sea."*

Bertrand Russell - *"War does not determine who is right, only who is left."*

Douglas MacArthur - *"The soldier above all others prays for peace, for it is the soldier who must suffer and bear the deepest wounds and scars of war."*

Mahatma Gandhi - *"A small body of determined spirits fired by an unquenchable faith in their mission can alter the course of history."*

Theodore Roosevelt - *"Never throughout history has a man who lived a life of ease left a name worth remembering."*

Arthur Koestler - *"Woe unto the defeated, whom history treads into the dust."*

Nicolas Chamfort, Maxims, and Considerations – "Almost the whole of history is but a sequence of horrors."

English Proverb - *"All that glitters is not gold."*

Alfred Lord Tennyson, The Charge of the Light Brigade –

"Half a league, half a League,

Half a league onward.

All in the valley of Death.

Rode the six hundred."

George Bernhard Shaw - *"We learn from experience that men never learn anything from experience."*

William James - *"History is a bath of blood."*

Stephen Crane, The Red Badge of Courage - *"It was not well to drive men into final corners; at those moments, they could all develop teeth and claws."*

Aristophanes - *"There is no honest man! Not one that can resist the attraction of gold!"*

Joseph Conrad, The Heart of Darkness - *"We penetrated deeper and deeper into the heart of darkness."*

William Hooke - *"A day of battle is a day of harvest for the devil."*

Munia Khan - *"Deep down inside, we always seek for our departed loved ones."*

Phillipe Perrin - *"It's only when you're flying above it that you realize how incredible that the earth really is."*

Rod Stewart - *"You go through life wondering what it is all about, but at the end of the day, it's family."*

Will Rogers - *"We can't all be heroes because somebody has to sit on the curb and clap as they go by."*

Printed in the United States
by Baker & Taylor Publisher Services